THREE PLAYS OF THE ABSURD

WALTER WYKES

Black Box Press
Los Angeles

Inquiries concerning amateur and professional performing rights for *The Father Clock* should be addressed to:

DRAMATIC PUBLISHING
P.O. Box 129, Woodstock, Illinois 60098

http://www.dramaticpublishing.com/

Inquiries concerning amateur and professional performing rights for *The Profession* and *Fading Joy* should be addressed to the author at: sandmaster@aol.com

The Profession © Walter Wykes, 1997; *Fading Joy* © Walter Wykes, 2000; *The Father Clock* © Walter Wykes, 1997.

ISBN 978-1-84728-405-1

First Edition

For Davey Marlin-Jones (1933-2004)

CONTENTS

THE PROFESSION

The Profession premiered at the Asylum Theatre in Las Vegas, Nevada on October 15, 1997, under the direction of Davey Marlin-Jones. The cast was as follows:

EUGENE: Bowd Beal
SCHÄFFER/VAGRANT: Eric Kaiser
ROSETTA/IBID: Jaylene Avena

SETTING:
A classroom, Eugene's apartment, the park

SCENE ONE:

[A classroom. EUGENE and ROSETTA sit in oversized school desks, their feet dangling high above the floor. They hold oversized pencils with oversized erasers and take notes on oversized tablets from an abnormally tall instructor, SCHÄFFER, dressed all in black, who stands about NINE FEET TALL! The two students recite as SCHÄFFER points to a diagram of the human intestines.]

                    SCHÄFFER
          [Pointing.]
Duodenum!

                    EUGENE/ROSETTA
Duodenum!

                    SCHÄFFER
          [Pointing.]
Jejunum!

                    EUGENE/ROSETTA
Jejunum!

                    SCHÄFFER
          [Pointing.]
Ileum!

EUGENE/ROSETTA

Ileum!

*[SCHÄFFER listens closely to the two students,
scrutinizes the position of their lips, the placement
of their tongues. He is determined not to let the
slightest mispronunciation escape unnoticed.]*

SCHÄFFER
[Pointing.]

Jejunum!

EUGENE/ROSETTA

Jejunum!

SCHÄFFER
[Pointing.]

Ileum!

EUGENE/ROSETTA

Ileum!

SCHÄFFER
[Pointing.]

Duodenum!

EUGENE/ROSETTA

Duodenum!

SCHÄFFER

Very good! As agents of The Profession, a thorough knowledge
of the human intestines can only serve you! Now ... Eugene!

[EUGENE rises. A harmless-looking little fellow, he tugs nervously at the collar of his spiffy new suit.]

What is this? This here.

[SCHÄFFER points to the diagram.]

EUGENE

Ahh ... that ... that there?

SCHÄFFER

Here. This little wormlike tube protruding from the cecum.

EUGENE

That ... ahh ...

[EUGENE studies the diagram carefully.]

That ...

[Pause. He continues to study the diagram.]

That would be the ... ahh ... little ... little ...

SCHÄFFER

Little wormlike ...

EUGENE

Little wormlike ... thing ... protruding ...

SCHÄFFER

From the ...

EUGENE

From the ...

[Pause.]

SCHÄFFER

Cecum.

EUGENE

Cecum.

[Pause.]

SCHÄFFER

Eugene?

EUGENE

Yes?

[SCHÄFFER taps the diagram.]

You know, I ... I don't think we went over that one. Did we go over that one? I don't think we did. I believe you ... ahh ... you skipped that one.

SCHÄFFER

Must you rely on me for *everything?*

EUGENE

Well ... I ... no ... but—

[SCHÄFFER taps the diagram.]

How am I supposed to know if you didn't—

SCHÄFFER

Throw yourself into the fire, Eugene! Hazard a guess!

EUGENE

A *guess?*

SCHÄFFER

That's right!

EUGENE

But--

SCHÄFFER

Go on!

EUGENE

Okay, but I—

SCHÄFFER

Eugene!

[SCHÄFFER threatens EUGENE with his stick.]

EUGENE

Is ... is it the ... ahh ... the duodenum?

SCHÄFFER

No.

EUGENE

Jejunum?

SCHÄFFER

No.

EUGENE

Ileum?

SCHÄFFER

No.

EUGENE

Well ... I ... I don't know then. I give up.
        [SCHÄFFER throws his hands in the air.]

SCHÄFFER

Good god!

EUGENE

Well, you never told us. How are we supposed to know if you never—

SCHÄFFER

Have you no intestines of your *own?!*
        [SCHÄFFER tears the diagram to shreds.
        EUGENE cowers in his desk.]

EUGENE
        [To ROSETTA.]
I ... I'm beginning to suspect he doesn't like me.

ROSETTA

Schäffer? Don't be ridiculous.
        [After a few moments, SCHÄFFER's rampage
        subsides. He pauses, takes a deep breath, then
        produces a second diagram identical to the first.
        Or perhaps he uses a freestanding chalkboard in
        which case he merely flips it around to reveal an
        identical drawing after savagely erasing the first.
        He points to the diagram.]

SCHÄFFER

Rosetta!

> *[ROSETTA stands. An attractive young woman with a very serious face, she is smartly dressed, hair pulled back neatly in a bun. She studies the diagram carefully.]*

ROSETTA

Vermiform appendix.

> *[Bells sound. Fireworks. EUGENE looks around, startled.]*

EUGENE

What ... what's going on?

SCHÄFFER

That is correct!

EUGENE

What's that sound?

SCHÄFFER

> *[With a grand, official air.]*

Congratulations, Rosetta—you have just been promoted to Level Two! Next promotion at 1000 points!

> *[ROSETTA claps gleefully.]*

EUGENE

Points? We ... we get *points?*

SCHÄFFER

Definition!

EUGENE

How do we get points?

ROSETTA

Narrow, wormlike tube protruding from the cecum, having no known useful function.

SCHÄFFER

No known useful function!

EUGENE

Could someone please explain the—

SCHÄFFER

A redundant organ!
        [SCHÄFFER begins to circle EUGENE.]
And if this ... *organ* ... this *redundant organ* ... this *waste* of tissue ... useless to the whole ... if this *organ* should become infected?! Inflamed?! An *irritation?!*
        [SCHÄFFER hovers over EUGENE menacingly.]
Eugene!

EUGENE

Ahhh ... wait! I ... I know this one! Ahhh ... Appendicitis! Inflammation of the ... of the vermiform—

SCHÄFFER

The diagnosis has been made! Procedure! Procedure!

EUGENE

Oh ... procedure. That ... that would be ... ahh ... appendectomy?

SCHÄFFER

Definition!

EUGENE

Excision of the vermiform appendix! Removal of the redundant organ to save the whole!

SCHÄFFER
[Still hovering menacingly.]
That is correct!
[A beat.]
Your progress continues to astound me ... *Eugene.*

EUGENE

Do I get any points?

SCHÄFFER
[Violently.]
SIT!!!
[EUGENE sits.]
You will now remove packet D-7 from your desks. As agents of The Profession, you will be entrusted with a sacred duty. An ancient task. In order to carry out this task, you must inspire confidence within the community. You must be beyond reproach! Trustworthy! The last suspected of any wrongdoing!
[A beat.]
Open your packets.

[EUGENE and ROSETTA open their packets and remove two very long, very dangerous-looking swords. These swords are much larger than the packets from which they have been removed. (ie. the old magician's suitcase illusion!) EUGENE is amazed by this and studies his packet carefully trying to figure out the trick. ROSETTA seems to take it for granted.]

You will now pair off and hurdle your partners instrument. Trust. Trust is the key.

EUGENE

Hurdle?

SCHÄFFER

That's right.

EUGENE

These?

SCHÄFFER

You may begin.

EUGENE
[Testing the blade.]
But ... someone could get hurt!

SCHÄFFER

The mysteries of The Profession are many and myriad, Eugene. If you wish to understand ... to fathom the depths ... you must have faith. You must throw yourself into the fire. Blindly.

ROSETTA

It's a test. We have to stick together.

EUGENE

But—

ROSETTA

Don't worry. I won't hurt you.

EUGENE

Why should I trust *you?* You're a complete stranger! And a *woman* on top of that!

ROSETTA

A *stranger?* But you've known me for years.

EUGENE

Have I?

ROSETTA

Yes. Since we were children.

EUGENE

Are you sure?

ROSETTA

We used to hunt frogs together.

EUGENE

That ... that was *you?*

ROSETTA

Our mothers were twins.

EUGENE

You're the frog girl?!

ROSETTA

Our fathers—hooked at the waist.

EUGENE

My God! This is fantastic!
                [EUGENE embraces her.]
What happened to you?! You vanished without a trace! One
moment we were hunting frogs, and the next—

ROSETTA

Shhh!

EUGENE

What?

ROSETTA

I can't talk about that.

EUGENE

About what?

ROSETTA

What happened.

EUGENE

Why not?

ROSETTA

It's forbidden.

EUGENE

Forbidden?

ROSETTA

That's right.

EUGENE

By whom?

ROSETTA

I'm not at liberty.
          [Pause.]
Shall we?

EUGENE

Well, I ... I don't know. It seems a bit dangerous.

ROSETTA

Do you want in or don't you?
          [EUGENE considers this.]

EUGENE

You know, now that I think about it—

ROSETTA

You do.

EUGENE

Do I?

ROSETTA

More than anything! You've dreamt of it all your life!

EUGENE

Oh ... well ... all right then. I suppose if ... if I've dreamt of it all my—

SCHÄFFER

You may begin!
> *[EUGENE extends his sword, and ROSETTA*
> *hurdles it easily.]*

Very good—switch.

ROSETTA

You see? It's not so bad.
> *[ROSETTA extends her instrument. EUGENE*
> *hurdles it carefully.]*

EUGENE

You're right! It's not so bad.

SCHÄFFER

Again.
> *[EUGENE hurdles the sword.]*

Again.
> *[Once more, EUGENE hurdles the weapon.]*

EUGENE

It's exhilarating! Life on the edge!

SCHÄFFER

Blindfolded!

EUGENE

What?

[*SCHÄFFER blindfolds EUGENE.*]

But I ... I can't see!

SCHÄFFER

[*A strange gleam in his eyes.*]

Precisely!

[*To ROSETTA.*]

Higher.

[*ROSETTA raises her weapon.*]

EUGENE

Higher?

[*SCHÄFFER pushes EUGENE towards the
sword.*]

How ... how much higher?!

SCHÄFFER

You may begin!

EUGENE

But—

SCHÄFFER

Begin! There's more at stake than meets the eye!

EUGENE

How ... how will I know when to jump?!

SCHÄFFER

Your partner will inform you.
>   *[Again, SCHÄFFER turns EUGENE towards the*
>   *sword.]*

Begin!

>   *[EUGENE approaches the sword very, very*
>   *slowly.]*

EUGENE

Okay ... ahh ... here ... here I come! I'm coming! I ... I must be
getting really ... really close ... tell me when to--

ROSETTA

Jump.

>   *[Pause. EUGENE does not budge.]*

EUGENE

A lot higher? Or just a little bit?

SCHÄFFER

Throw yourself! Blindly!

EUGENE

But—

SCHÄFFER

Blindly! Into the fire!

ROSETTA

Trust me.

SCHÄFFER

The chasm!

ROSETTA

Jump.

     [EUGENE hesitates.]

Jump!

     [EUGENE safely hurdles the instrument.]

SCHÄFFER

Damn!

EUGENE

What was that?! What did he just say?!
     [EUGENE removes his blindfold.]

ROSETTA

What did *who* say?

EUGENE

Schäffer!

ROSETTA

He didn't say anything.

EUGENE

Yes, he did! Didn't you hear?!

ROSETTA

Hear what? It's your mind playing tricks.

[SCHÄFFER tears the second diagram to shreds.]

EUGENE

He ... he didn't want me to make it! He was hoping I'd impale myself!

ROSETTA

Don't be ridiculous. He's a great educator. A respected member of The Profession.
> *[SCHÄFFER composes himself. Returns to his desk.]*

SCHÄFFER

You may remove packet E-2 from your desks.

EUGENE
> *[To ROSETTA.]*

What's in this one—hand-grenades?!
> *[EUGENE produces a packet. ROSETTA comes up empty-handed. She raises her hand.]*

SCHÄFFER

Rosetta!

ROSETTA

I don't have an E-2. I have a 1-X ...
> *[She removes a dangerous-looking package from her desk.]*

SCHÄFFER

No! No ... that must only be opened in extreme situations. As a last resort. The handbook makes it very clear. You'll have to share with Eugene.

[To EUGENE.]
Well ... open the packet!

> *[EUGENE opens his packet, and, as if by magic, a stream of oversized, brightly-colored condoms begin to spew endlessly into the air. There seems to be an unlimited supply—far too many to have ever fit into the packet from which they issue forth.]*

EUGENE

What ... what are these?

ROSETTA

Condoms. Prophylactics. Common birth control device. Also known as *rubbers, skins* or *bags.*

EUGENE

Yes, but what ... what are they for?

ROSETTA

You don't *know?*

EUGENE

No, I ... I know what they're *for*, but I don't—

SCHÄFFER

You will now pair off and perform the carnal act of possession. Ten minutes. You may begin.

> *[Pause. EUGENE raises his hand.]*

What now?

EUGENE

Well, I ... I just have a question. When you say *perform the carnal act* ... do you ... ahh ... do you actually mean ... ... well, what ... what do you mean exactly?

SCHÄFFER

Sexual intercourse.

EUGENE

Ahhh.

SCHÄFFER

You may begin.
> [*SCHÄFFER produces a stopwatch and proceeds to time them. An awkward pause. Once more, EUGENE raises his hand.*]

EUGENE

I have a wife.

SCHÄFFER

Even so.

EUGENE

We've only just married.

SCHÄFFER

So much the better.

EUGENE

But—

SCHÄFFER

You may begin!
>*[Pause.]*

EUGENE

I ... I really don't think I can.
>*[SCHÄFFER pauses his stopwatch. He*
>*approaches EUGENE, attempting to contain his*
>*mounting rage.]*

SCHÄFFER

Eugene ... may I call you *Eugene?*

EUGENE

Well ... sure. Sure. If you'd like.

SCHÄFFER

As an agent of The Profession, you will frequently be exposed to
the naked body. Heads. Buttocks. Ankles. Breasts.

ROSETTA

Testicles.

SCHÄFFER

You must become deadened to them. Numb. Numb, numb,
numb! How would it reflect on The Profession if you were to
become aroused on the job? Hmmm? That wouldn't be proper
at all, now would it?

EUGENE

Well ... no ... I ... I never thought of it like that.

SCHÄFFER

Exactly!

EUGENE

But—

SCHÄFFER

Do you want to embarrass us all?

EUGENE

No. No, I don't. Of course not.

SCHÄFFER

Very well. You may begin.
          [SCHÄFFER restarts his stopwatch.]
Ten minutes.

EUGENE
[To ROSETTA.]
What ... ahh ... what do you think?

ROSETTA

Hmmm?

EUGENE

Intercourse. It seems a bit unusual.

ROSETTA

Oh, no.

EUGENE

No?

ROSETTA

Not at all. It's quite standard.

EUGENE

Really? I had no idea.

ROSETTA

All the top programs require it. Haven't you read the handbook?

EUGENE

What handbook?

ROSETTA

The handbook.

EUGENE

I ... I haven't seen any handbook.

ROSETTA

It's a crucial element of the training. The ability to control one's natural desires. It's what separates us from the apes.

SCHÄFFER

I find your hesitation disturbing, young man. One might begin to question your commitment.

ROSETTA

We have to stick together.

EUGENE

Apparently.

SCHÄFFER

The Profession requires quick thinking! Split-second decisions!

EUGENE

But—

SCHÄFFER

No "buts!"

EUGENE

But my wife, Ibid—

ROSETTA

Oh, what a beautiful name!

EUGENE

Thank you. She's very sensitive about these things, and, you know, we ... we've only just married. This morning.

ROSETTA

Oh! Congratulations!

EUGENE

Thank you. We ... we haven't even ... well ... you know ...

SCHÄFFER

Perhaps you should examine your priorities!

EUGENE

My ... well ... no ... I—

SCHÄFFER

How do you think she'd feel if you were booted out?! Hmmm?!

EUGENE

Booted out?

SCHÄFFER

That's right! How do you think she'd feel about that?! Your sensitive young wife!

EUGENE

I ... I don't—

SCHÄFFER

Chained forever to a failure! A reject! The Mark of shame upon her forehead! And her children's! And her children's children's! Think of the humiliation! The disgrace! She wouldn't like that at all—now would she?!

EUGENE

Well ... no.

SCHÄFFER

Ten minutes. You may begin.
        [SCHÄFFER restarts his stopwatch.]

EUGENE

It's just that I—

ROSETTA

Think of her. The poor thing.

EUGENE

But—

SCHÄFFER

DO YOU WANT IN OR DON'T YOU?!!!

EUGENE

Well ... I ... I suppose I must or I—

ROSETTA

You do. You've dreamt of it—

EUGENE

—all my life, that's right. Perhaps we could just imagine! Or ...
or beat each other with sticks!

SCHÄFFER

Don't be absurd.

ROSETTA

Well ... shall we?

> *[She hands EUGENE a condom. He accepts it*
> *reluctantly—studies it. Picks up another. And*
> *another.]*

EUGENE

Wait a minute ... look at this ... they're ... they're all ... they're
full of holes! All of them! Look! Someone's taken a needle to
them!

SCHÄFFER

Of course.

ROSETTA

What did you expect?

SCHÄFFER

They've been specially prepared.

EUGENE

But ... they've ... they've got holes! They're useless!

SCHÄFFER

Precisely.

EUGENE

What if I catch something and die?!

SCHÄFFER
[A strange gleam in his eyes.]
That's always a possibility!

ROSETTA

Don't worry. You're safe with me.

EUGENE

How can you be sure?! I mean ... you know ... the ... the way
things are nowadays—

ROSETTA

I'm a virgin.

EUGENE

A virgin! Hah!

ROSETTA

That's right.

EUGENE
[Disbelief.]

No!

ROSETTA

Yes.

EUGENE
[Tempted.]
Really?

ROSETTA

A monument to purity. A living shrine, completely untouched
by human hands.
[Pause—EUGENE considers this.]

EUGENE

Completely?
[She nods.]
Completely untouched?

ROSETTA

Completely.
[Pause. EUGENE considers this.]

EUGENE

Not ... not touched at all?

ROSETTA

That's right.
[Pause. EUGENE considers this.]

EUGENE

And you want me to ... ahh ...

ROSETTA

I'm only thinking of The Profession.
[Pause. EUGENE considers this.]

EUGENE

Can you prove it? I mean, you know, that you're a—

ROSETTA

A virgin? Of course. Just ask my husband.

EUGENE

Your husband?

ROSETTA

That's right.

EUGENE

Oh—I suppose he's a virgin, too!

ROSETTA

Oh, no. Not at all. That's why he proposed. My husband is very experienced. He's been with hundreds of women. Thousands. On our wedding day alone, he impregnated seven bridesmaids, two caterers, the photographer, the photographer's assistant, her youngest daughter, the preacher's wife, my third-grade English teacher, a marine biologist, two blue whales, and one old woman who just happened to wander in off the street. He has no morals, you see. He thinks they're very old fashioned. He's a philosopher! But he liked the idea of having a virgin, you know, tarnishing the flower, plucking the petal, all that—it was very exciting for him. Unfortunately, he knew, being a philosopher, that the moment he actually did it, everything would be ruined. So as soon as the ceremony was over, he locked me away in a little room with his galoshes.

EUGENE

That ... that's awful!

ROSETTA

Yes. In addition, he had a problem with his feet. A certain ... odor ... and the galoshes ... well ... you know. I used to beg him to release me. To have his way. Or at least put a bullet through my head. But he wouldn't do it. Except on Sundays. On Sundays, he often let me out, and we would pretend to be very happy.

EUGENE

So ... what happened?

ROSETTA
[Violently.]
NOTHING! I DON'T KNOW WHAT YOU'RE TALKING
ABOUT! I'M COMPLETELY INNOCENT!

EUGENE
What? I ... no—

ROSETTA
Oh ... you ... you only meant ...
[A disarming little laugh.]
No one knows. One Sunday, we went for a little stroll in the
park and he just ... disappeared. Vanished without a trace. His
body was never found.

EUGENE
My god! He ... he just vanished?!

ROSETTA
Strange things have been known to happen in that park. Evil
things. I'd stay away from there if I were you.

EUGENE
How do you ... ahh ... how do you know ... if ... if his body was
never found ... I mean ... how do you know he's dead?

ROSETTA
[A strange gleam in her eyes.]
Oh ... just a hunch.

[ROSETTA and SCHÄFFER exchange a meaningful glance. They begin to chuckle, softly at first, but it soon grows into harsh, raucous laughter. EUGENE stares at them, horrified.]

EUGENE

Oh my god! You ... you killed him!

ROSETTA

Oh, now don't get hysterical.

EUGENE

You killed him! Your own husband! Murder! Help!
[EUGENE tries to flee, but SCHÄFFER intercepts him and returns him to his seat.]

ROSETTA

Let's get on with it—shall we?
[ROSETTA begins to shed her clothes.]

EUGENE

Please! I can't! She'll ... she'll eat me alive! Like a spider!
Help! Help! Someone help me!

SCHÄFFER

Ten minutes.

EUGENE

[Frantically.]
Wait! Wait! What if ... ahh ... what if *I* have something?!

SCHÄFFER

You?

EUGENE

Yes!

[SCHÄFFER laughs.]

SCHÄFFER

Hah! What do *you* have?

EUGENE

A disease!

SCHÄFFER

Which one?

EUGENE

The worst kind! It's very contagious!

ROSETTA

I've been vaccinated.

EUGENE

It's a new strain! A mutation!

ROSETTA

For the sake of The Profession, I'm willing to take that risk.

[ROSETTA stands naked before them.]

SCHÄFFER

Oh! How noble you are! What a magnificent creature! Look at her, Eugene!

[EUGENE attempts to avert his eyes.]

LOOK AT HER!!!
> *[EUGENE complies—half resisting, half*
> *fascinated.]*

Isn't she exquisite?! Let this be a lesson to you! Put aside your
selfish nature! Think of The Profession!

ROSETTA

Think of your wife. Do it for her, if nothing else.

EUGENE

But—

SCHÄFFER

You may begin!

EUGENE

It's just that I—

SCHÄFFER

Ten minutes!

EUGENE

But—

SCHÄFFER

Begin!
> *[SCHÄFFER restarts his stopwatch. Blackout.]*

* * *

SCENE TWO:

[A very small apartment. In sharp contrast to the oversized classroom, everything here is in miniature –including the walls which are composed of brightly-colored plastic. The couch is barely large enough for one adult. The dining room table looks like a child's play thing—as do many of the other items including the telephone, clock, television set, kitchen sink, etc... The effect is that of a "play house." After a moment, the door— which is scarcely three feet tall—swings open. EUGENE crawls into the room on his hands and knees. He is out of breath and perspiring heavily.]

EUGENE
[To himself.]
Okay ... okay ... only one thing to do!

IBID
[Offstage.]
Eugene?
[EUGENE freezes.]
Eugene! Is that you?!

EUGENE
Yes! It's me!
[EUGENE begins to dart nervously about the room.]

All right ... out with it! Right up front! That's all there is to it!
Honesty is the best—

IBID

How was your first day?!

EUGENE

My ... my first day?!
>   *[EUGENE stumbles over the couch.]*

IBID

Your first day! How was it?!

EUGENE

Ahh ... fine ... fine! It was fine! Just fine! Normal! Just a
normal day!

IBID

Are you all right?!
>   *[EUGENE frantically attempts to put the tiny
>   couch back in its place.]*

EUGENE

What?!

IBID

I said, "Are you all right?!"

EUGENE

Oh! Yes! Fine!

IBID

Is something wrong?!

EUGENE

No! No! Everything's fine! Just fine! Normal! Why do you ask?!

IBID

You sound a little nervous!

EUGENE

Me?!
              [A nervous little laugh.]
No! No! Not nervous at all!
              [Enter IBID. She looks exactly like ROSETTA except that her hair is styled in a much more conservative manner. She resembles the perfect housewife in every way. She wears a conservative house dress, an apron, and a pair of yellow dishwashing gloves. She carries a brightly-colored package.]

IBID

Surprise!

EUGENE

What ... what's that?

IBID

A present!

EUGENE

A present? For me?

IBID

That's right! A reward! For all of your hard work! Your dedication!

EUGENE

Oh ... well, I ... I'm not ... I'm not really in the mood for a present right now.

IBID

Why not?

EUGENE

Well, I ... I don't deserve it.

IBID

What do you mean?

EUGENE

What do I mean? I mean, I haven't done anything special.

IBID

Oh poo! You're my little practitioner!

EUGENE

Yes, *well* ...

IBID

What?
                [An awkward pause.]
Oh, god! What is it, Eugene?! What have you done?! Did you get expelled?! Booted out?!

EUGENE

No! No ...

IBID

Oh, thank Heavens! You had me worried there for a minute!

EUGENE

It's just that I ... I've been thinking.

IBID

[Alarmed.]

Thinking?

EUGENE

Yes.

IBID

Here!

[She hands him the present—a distraction.]

EUGENE

Let's run away together!

IBID

What?

EUGENE

Let's run away!

IBID

Run away?

EUGENE

Yes! To an island somewhere! Someplace far off! With ... with lots of fish!

IBID

Fish?

EUGENE

That's right!

IBID

Oh, I ... I don't think that's a good idea.
   [IBID begins to wander aimlessly, deeply
   disturbed, straightening as she goes.]
Fish are such filthy little creatures, prowling about in the darkness and the mud, eating their neighbors without a second thought—that's no way for the children to grow up.

EUGENE

What children?

IBID

Our children.

EUGENE

Our children?

IBID

That's right.

                    EUGENE

But we ... we don't have any children.
          [A beat.]
Do we?

                    IBID

No ... but it's only a matter of time! We'll have some sooner or
later!
          [She begins to scrub the kitchen table viciously.]

                    EUGENE

Just think. We could run naked in the sand all day and ... and
collect seashells! And play with the dolphins! Dolphins are
very civilized! They don't eat each other! We could learn their
language! The language of the sea! We could sleep under the
moon with our dolphin friends and—

                    IBID

I don't want to run away! I'm perfectly content!
          [Pause.]

                    EUGENE

Ibid ... there's ... there's something I have to tell you.

                    IBID

Not now!

                    EUGENE

What?

IBID

Not now! I'm busy!

EUGENE

But—

IBID

Can't you see I'm scrubbing the table! There! Finished! Open
your present!

EUGENE

But there's something I want to—

IBID

Open it!

EUGENE

But—

IBID

Now!
               [He does.]
It's a plaque. "An agent of The Profession must display his
credentials in a prominent position so as to appear above
reproach." I read it in the handbook.

EUGENE

The *handbook?*

IBID

That's right.

EUGENE
[A little too casually.]
What ... ahh ... which ... which handbook?

IBID
The handbook. You know.

EUGENE
No! I don't know! I never saw any handbook!

IBID
You don't like it.

EUGENE
No, I like it fine. It's just that—

IBID
Good! Now tell me about your day!

EUGENE
[Begins to fidget.]
My ... ahh ... my day?

IBID
That's right. You may begin.

EUGENE
What?

IBID

You may begin. You have ... ten minutes.

> *[IBID pulls a stopwatch from her apron and*
> *proceeds to time him.]*

Go on.

EUGENE

What are you—

IBID

Begin!

EUGENE

Well ... there ... there isn't much to tell really. It was just a day.
Just a day. Like any other day. You know. Well ... time to hit
the hay!

IBID

Sit.

> *[He does.]*

I want all the details.

EUGENE

> *[Uneasily.]*

All of them?

IBID

That's right.

> *[Pause.]*

                              EUGENE
Egypt! We could go to Egypt! We could live in the pyramids!
And ... and talk to the ... ahh ... crocodiles! The crocodiles! We
could ride on their backs and—

                              IBID
The *pyramids?*

                              EUGENE
Yes!

                              IBID
Haven't you heard?

                              EUGENE
Heard what?

                              IBID
What happened.

                              EUGENE
No. Did something happen?

                              IBID
They're gone.

                              EUGENE
What?

IBID

The pyramids.

EUGENE

No!

IBID

Yes.

EUGENE

They ... they can't be!

IBID

They've crumbled. All of them. Every last one.

EUGENE

My god!

IBID

Yes. It's a terrible disaster. Everyone's very upset. There's a
relief fund being set up. We should send a few dollars.

EUGENE

But ... how can that be?! The pyramids have been around for
thousands of years! They can't just ... crumble! When did it
happen?

IBID

This morning. Now, tell me about your day or I'm going to put a
bullet through your head.
        [A disarming little laugh.]

EUGENE
[Unnerved.]
What?

IBID
I said, "Tell me about your day or I'm going to put a bullet through your head."
[A disarming little laugh.]

EUGENE
What's gotten into you?!

IBID
Nothing. I'm only trying to be a good wife.

EUGENE
Well ... all right ... that's ... that's what I wanted to talk to you about actually. My day. You see ... there ... there was this girl.

IBID
A girl?

EUGENE
That's right. And there was something about her. I couldn't put my finger on it, but ... she seemed strangely familiar.

ROSETTA
Familiar?
[Tugging nervously at her wig.]
In ... in what way?

EUGENE

Well ... it was almost as if ... as if I'd seen her somewhere before, you know? As if I'd known her my whole life.

IBID

That's ridiculous!

EUGENE

Yes, but, well, it turns out I *have* known her my whole life! When we were kids, we used to hunt frogs together!

IBID

Eugene ... you know very well that every woman you've ever met has claimed to be your frog girl. It's the oldest trick in the book.

EUGENE

Yes, but ... our mothers were twins!

IBID

Twins? Is that right?

EUGENE

Yes! Isn't it remarkable?!

IBID

I never knew your mother had a twin.

EUGENE

She doesn't.
            [Pause.]
Oh ... that's strange.

IBID

What else?

EUGENE

What?

IBID

Your day! Your day! Tell me about your day!

EUGENE

Oh. Well, we ... we opened a lot of packages.

IBID

Packages?

EUGENE

Yes. Packages.

IBID

Were they *secret* packages?

EUGENE

I ... I don't know. They might have been.

IBID

What was inside?
                    [EUGENE fidgets.]

EUGENE

If they were secret packages, perhaps I shouldn't tell you.

IBID

Eugene!

EUGENE

Swords! They were full of swords! Great big ones!

IBID

What *else?*

EUGENE

Oh ... mostly swords.
        [An awkward pause.]
Cleveland! What about Cleveland?! We could move to
Cleveland!

IBID

Did you fall on your head? Did you have some kind of
accident?

EUGENE

No, it's just that I ... I don't feel like we *belong* here. This place
doesn't fit us at all!

IBID

What do you mean?

EUGENE

Well ... take this couch for instance. Doesn't it seem a bit ... well
... *unusual?*

IBID

Unusual?

EUGENE

Yes.

IBID

The couch?

EUGENE

Yes!

> *[She examines the miniature couch.]*

IBID

In what way?

EUGENE

Take a good look.
> *[She does.]*

IBID

Give me a hint.

EUGENE

Think proportionately.
> *[IBID studies the couch. Pause.]*

IBID

I don't see it.

EUGENE

No?

IBID

No.

EUGENE

Not at all? You don't find it a bit ... odd?
            [Again, she studies the couch.]

IBID

Not at all.

EUGENE

And these walls? This window? The telephone?

IBID

What about it?

EUGENE

Try to make a call!
            [She does.]

IBID

The lines must be down.

EUGENE

They're *always* down!

IBID

Not necessarily. Perhaps they're only down when you try to
make a call.

EUGENE

Don't you think that's suspicious?!

IBID

Come here.

EUGENE

Why?

IBID

I want to feel your forehead.

EUGENE

I'm perfectly sane!

IBID

Why haven't you ever said anything about this before?

EUGENE

Well ... I ... I've suspected something all along, but I couldn't be sure, so I kept my mouth shut. Only now my eyes have been opened! I don't know how it happened, but I'm seeing things clearly for the first time!

IBID

How do you know you weren't seeing things clearly before?

EUGENE

Listen to me! We have to get out of here!

IBID

I don't want to get out of here. I'm perfectly content.

EUGENE

But they're playing us for fools!

IBID

Who is?

EUGENE

Well, I ... I don't know. I haven't figured that part out yet. But I'm working on it!

IBID

What about The Profession? If we leave now, they'll never take you back.

EUGENE

I don't care!

IBID

But ... it's what you've always dreamed of.

EUGENE

Not anymore! I've had it with The Profession! I'm my own man!

IBID

Shhh! Don't say that! Have you lost your mind!
[IBID draws the curtains and bolts the door.]

EUGENE

Ah-hah!

IBID

What?

EUGENE

Why did you do that?!

IBID

Do what?

EUGENE

Draw the curtains and bolt the door!

IBID

I felt a little draft. Didn't you feel it?

EUGENE

No!

IBID

Would you like some tea?
> *[IBID produces a tiny tea set from the cupboard.]*

EUGENE

What about the door?!

IBID

Tea always makes you feel better.
> *[She arranges the tiny saucers and begins to pour*
> *imaginary tea from a small pitcher.]*

EUGENE

A draft doesn't explain the door!

IBID

One lump or two?

EUGENE

Why bolt the door if it's just a draft?!
   [IBID puts two imaginary lumps of sugar in
   EUGENE's cup.]

IBID

There. I know how you like your sugar. Now drink up.
   [She hands him an empty cup.]

EUGENE

But there isn't any—

IBID

Go on.

EUGENE

But—

IBID

Drink!
   [EUGENE pretends to drink from the tiny cup.]
Now ... don't you feel better?

EUGENE

No! No, I don't feel better! It's empty!

IBID

What do you mean?

EUGENE

What do you mean what do I mean?! My cup's empty! There's no tea!

IBID

Of course not—you just drank it.

EUGENE

No! I never had any to begin with! It's PRETEND tea!

IBID

Don't be ridiculous. Do you want some more?

EUGENE

No! No, I don't want any—oh nevermind!
          [IBID rises and carries the tea set to the sink.]
Look ... Ibid ... there ... there are *things,* okay? Certain ... *things* ... which ... which you couldn't possibly understand! All right? Certain *inconsistencies* one must agree to overlook if one intends to succeed in this business! Weights one must carry! Games that must be played! "Jump through these hoops! Do this! Do that! Don't ask any questions! Don't complain! Be good boys and girls! Pretend!"

IBID

What on earth are you talking about?

EUGENE

This couch ...

IBID

Yes?

EUGENE

It's not a couch!

IBID

Of course it's a—

EUGENE

And the phone—it's a toy! I child's play-thing! These walls—I could knock them down if I wanted!

IBID

Don't you dare!

EUGENE

It's a farce! A lie! I won't pretend anymore! Today, they ... they asked me to do something.

IBID
[Suddenly spellbound.]
The Profession?!

EUGENE

Yes. They asked me to complete a ... a certain *task*.

IBID

A certain task!

EUGENE

That's right. A certain task which I didn't want to do! I fought it tooth and nail! But they wouldn't give in! They insisted this task be carried out!

IBID

This *task* ...

EUGENE

Yes?

IBID

Was it the carnal act?
        [Pause.]

EUGENE

How ... how did you know that?

IBID

I read it in the handbook.

EUGENE

The handbook?

IBID

That's right.
        [EUGENE sits in stunned silence.]

EUGENE

Where is it?

IBID

What?

EUGENE

The handbook. Where is it? I want to see.

IBID

I don't remember. I ... I must have misplaced it.

EUGENE

Well, it must be here somewhere! What does it look like?

IBID

Did you?

EUGENE

What?

IBID

Complete the task?

EUGENE

[Searching for the handbook.]

Oh! No! No, I stood my ground! I refused! They locked me in a tiny closet, fed me nothing but bread and water, and told me to get my priorities in order, but I escaped! And I'm not going back! I've won! I stood up to them! I thought of you, and I didn't give in!

IBID

[Furious.]

What?!

EUGENE

I ... I didn't give in.

IBID

Why *not?!*

EUGENE

Huh?

IBID

Why not?! Do you think I've had to do any less?! Do you think I haven't had to make certain compromises?! Ignore certain *inconsistencies?!* Hike up my skirt every now and then?!

EUGENE

You?

IBID

Of course! Don't be naive!

EUGENE

But ... I ... I thought—

IBID

Tomorrow morning, you will march right back in there, and you will apologize for your behavior! You will tell them you've got your priorities in order, that you are committed to The Profession, and you will complete the task! Is that clear?!
        [Pause.]
Is it?!

[EUGENE nods.]

Good!

[IBID rises and begins to tidy up. EUGENE sits silently for a long moment, unable to speak. Finally...]

EUGENE

Ibid ...

IBID

[Sharply.]

What?!

EUGENE

May I ... may I have some tea?
[Pause.]

IBID

Some *tea?*

EUGENE

That's right.
[She softens.]

IBID

Of course.

[She pours EUGENE an imaginary cup of tea.]

EUGENE

Thank you.

[IBID hovers over EUGENE. As he begins to drink the non-existent tea, darkness slowly envelops them.]

* * *

SCENE THREE:

*[The classroom--next day. EUGENE and
ROSETTA sit in their desks in a kind of daze, their
clothes half-buttoned, their hair mussed, their faces
smeared with lipstick. SCHÄFFER hovers over
them with a clipboard.]*

SCHÄFFER
[To EUGENE.]
Well ... how do you feel?

EUGENE
[Lost in a dream.]
Hmmm?

SCHÄFFER
How do you feel? Deadened?

EUGENE
Hmmm? Oh. I ... I don't know.
[Pause. He grins.]
Different.

SCHÄFFER
Numb?

EUGENE
No.

SCHÄFFER
[*Irritated.*]
No?

EUGENE
[*Enraptured.*]
No ... no, I don't think so!

SCHÄFFER
Hmmm ...
[*SCHÄFFER makes some notes on his clipboard—turns to ROSETTA.*]
What about you? Deadened?
[*No response. SCHÄFFER snaps his fingers, but still she does not respond. In contrast to EUGENE's haze of delight, ROSETTA's face is glazed over with an expression of boredom, disappointment, and revulsion. SCHÄFFER makes a few notes.*]

EUGENE
I ... I have a suggestion.

SCHÄFFER
A *suggestion?*

EUGENE
That's right.

SCHÄFFER

Well ... let's have it.

EUGENE

Perhaps we should try it again.

SCHÄFFER

Try it again?

EUGENE

Yes!

SCHÄFFER

Oh, that won't be necessary.

EUGENE

But ... I think I might have the beginnings of numbness! See! Right here! In my thumb! A little tingling! One more time might do it!

SCHÄFFER

No, no, we have other methods.

EUGENE

Other methods?

SCHÄFFER

That's right.

EUGENE

What's wrong with this method? I mean, why move on until we've exhausted the present course? We could be on the verge of a breakthrough! No, no, I'm not prepared to give up just yet. In fact, I'm firmly opposed to it!

SCHÄFFER

Your partner seems to have had enough.

EUGENE

Yes, but ... what if she's only *temporarily* deadened? Did you think of that? She could snap out of it at any moment! Then where would we be?

> [ROSETTA shudders, re-living some unpleasant experience.]

There! You see!

SCHÄFFER

Hmmm ...

> [He studies ROSETTA—makes a few more notes.]

EUGENE

Once more for good measure. I'm only thinking of The Profession.

SCHÄFFER

I'm afraid not.

EUGENE

No?

SCHÄFFER

The handbook strictly forbids it.

EUGENE

The handbook?

SCHÄFFER

That's right.

EUGENE

But I ... I thought the handbook *required* it.

SCHÄFFER

That was before. Things have changed.

EUGENE

How? In what way? When did they change?

SCHÄFFER

I can't tell you.

EUGENE

Why not?

SCHÄFFER

It's forbidden.

EUGENE

Forbidden!

SCHÄFFER

That's right.

EUGENE

By whom?

SCHÄFFER

[Horrified.]

WHAT?!

EUGENE

By whom? Who does the forbidding? Is it one person or is there, you know, some sort of panel?

SCHÄFFER

It's not your place to question!

EUGENE

Why not?

SCHÄFFER

Return to your desk!

EUGENE

All right, look, just give me a hint.

SCHÄFFER

A *hint?*

EUGENE

That's right! A little clue!

SCHÄFFER

Who do you think you are?! Return to your desk at once!

EUGENE

Are clues specifically forbidden—or just straight answers?
[SCHÄFFER hesitates.]
Ah-hah! They're not! Clues are allowed! Come on! Out with
it! Forbidden by whom? Don't try to hold out on me or I'll ...
I'll make a scene! I'll question your integrity as an instructor!
File official complaints! Do you want that on your record?

SCHÄFFER

I've followed the handbook to the letter!

EUGENE

Are you *sure?*

SCHÄFFER

Of course!

EUGENE

To the *letter?*

SCHÄFFER

I've studied that book from top to bottom! Memorized each
passage!

EUGENE

Even so, most complaints, you know, aren't won or lost on their own merits, but rather on larger issues—politics and the position of the planets. In this day and age, you never know what could happen!

SCHÄFFER

Nonsense!

EUGENE

Perhaps there's some passage you've forgotten.

SCHÄFFER

Impossible!

EUGENE

Something obscure.

SCHÄFFER

Never!

EUGENE

An addendum.
            [Again, SCHÄFFER hesitates.]
Do you really want to take the chance?

SCHÄFFER

I ... I don't suppose one little clue could hurt. But don't ask for anything more!

[SCHÄFFER removes his hat and offers it to
EUGENE--motions for him to look inside.
EUGENE reaches into the hat and pulls out an
orange.]

EUGENE

It's ... an orange.
        [SCHÄFFER nods expectantly.]
This is my clue? An *orange?* That's it?! This orange is
supposed to tell me who's running the show? Who's doing all
the forbidding? The great Forbidder!
        [SCHÄFFER nods—motions as if to say, "Go on—
        think about it!" EUGENE studies the orange
        carefully.]
An *orange picker?*
        [SCHÄFFER indicates that this is incorrect.]
A magician!
        [Again, wrong. SCHÄFFER waits expectantly.]
I have no idea.

SCHÄFFER

Throw yourself into the fire, Eugene! Hazard a guess!
        [EUGENE studies the orange with renewed
        determination. SCHÄFFER hovers over him
        hopefully. Occasionally, they exchange a
        meaningful glance. Slowly, however, EUGENE's
        determination begins to wane.]

EUGENE

Give me another clue.

[*SCHÄFFER throws his hands up in despair.*]
Well, how am I supposed to know if no one ever—
    [*ROSETTA comes to with a start.*]

ROSETTA

Oh!
    [*She spies EUGENE and, although she smiles at
    him awkwardly, seems a little revolted.*]

SCHÄFFER

How do you feel?

ROSETTA

Deadened. Numb.
    [*Bells sound. Fireworks.*]

SCHÄFFER

Good. That's one at least.
    [*With a grand, official air.*]
Congratulations, Rosetta—you have just been promoted to Level
Three! Next promotion at 10,000 points!

EUGENE

Hey! Wait a minute! How did she get so many points?! I did
all the work!

SCHÄFFER

Pfff!
    [*EUGENE shows ROSETTA his orange.*]

EUGENE

Look at this orange. Take a good look. What do you see? All I
see is an orange, but there's something more. It's a clue.

ROSETTA
[Still a little revolted.]
To what?

EUGENE

The mastermind behind it all!

ROSETTA

Ahh.
[She studies the orange.]
An orange picker?

EUGENE

I've already guessed that.

ROSETTA

Hmmm ...
[They study the orange.]
A fruit fly?

EUGENE

A fruit fly?

ROSETTA

That's right.

EUGENE

An insect?

ROSETTA

Why not?

EUGENE

But it's brain would be the size of a ...
          [Pause. EUGENE considers this.]
Then again, when you look around ...
          [To SCHÄFFER.]
A fruit fly?

SCHÄFFER
          [Alarmed.]
What's that?

EUGENE

I ... I said "fruit fly".

SCHÄFFER

Return to your desks!

EUGENE

What? But I—

SCHÄFFER

Return to your desk! No more games!

EUGENE

I only said—

SCHÄFFER

Take your seat this instant!
    [He does.]

EUGENE

    [To ROSETTA.]
This fruit-fly thing is really getting to him! There must be
something to it!

SCHÄFFER

    [Fumbling through his notes.]
Open ... ahh ... open packet ... packet 1-X!
    [ROSETTA removes the dangerous-looking packet
    from her desk. EUGENE searches his desk but
    comes up empty. He raises his hand.]
Not now.

EUGENE

But I don't—

SCHÄFFER

Silence!
    [SCHÄFFER pulls a handkerchief from thin air
    and wipes his brow.]
Go on! Open the package!

[ROSETTA opens the package and removes a large pair of hedge clippers. Once again, the clippers are much larger than the packet from which they are removed.]

EUGENE

Oh, that's nothing. Hah! After yesterday? A little pair of clippers? Pfff! You hold them—I'll go first.

SCHÄFFER

These are not for hurdling.

EUGENE

Not for hurdling?

SCHÄFFER

No.

EUGENE

What ... ahh ... what are they for?

SCHÄFFER
                    [To ROSETTA.]
He isn't numb.

ROSETTA

Not numb?

SCHÄFFER

No.

ROSETTA

My god!

*[SCHÄFFER takes the clippers from ROSETTA.
Tests them.]*

EUGENE

You know, I'm ... I'm a little numb ... my ... my thumb ... see ... a
little tingling ... actually, it's ... it's my whole ... my whole arm ...
I hadn't noticed before, but really my whole left side!

SCHÄFFER

Do you take us for fools?

EUGENE

Fools? No, I—

SCHÄFFER
[To ROSETTA.]
You will perform the operation.

ROSETTA
[A strange gleam in her eyes.]
Of course.

EUGENE

The *operation?*

ROSETTA

Testicals!

[ROSETTA takes the clippers. Tests them.]

EUGENE

Oh! There it goes! My whole body! Numb! It's a delayed reaction! I told you I'd come around!

[ROSETTA approaches EUGENE with the clippers.]

Now ... now hold on! Wait just a minute!

SCHÄFFER

As an agent of The Profession, you will be entrusted with a sacred duty. An ancient task. In order to carry out this task, you must inspire confidence within the community. You must be beyond reproach. Trustworthy. The last suspected of any wrongdoing.

EUGENE

But—

SCHÄFFER

Trust. Trust is the key.

[To ROSETTA.]

You may begin.

EUGENE

But someone could get hurt! Me!

SCHÄFFER

The mysteries of The Profession are many and myriad, Eugene. If you wish to understand ... to fathom the depths ... you must have faith.

EUGENE

I don't want to fathom! Somebody else can fathom! *You*
fathom!

ROSETTA

It's a test. We have to stick together.

SCHÄFFER

What if you were to become aroused on the job? That wouldn't
be proper at all, now would it? Do you want to embarrass us all?
[ROSETTA tests the clippers.]

EUGENE

Stay back!

SCHÄFFER

You must become deadened! Numb! Numb! Numb!

EUGENE

Don't come any closer! I'm warning you!

SCHÄFFER

Don't be frightened. In a moment, it will all be over.

EUGENE

I don't want it to be over!

SCHÄFFER

Everything will go much smoother if you just relax. Struggling
only makes things worse. Messy. You'll force us to improvise.

[ROSETTA takes a swipe at EUGENE with the clippers. EUGENE screams. SCHÄFFER waves his handkerchief in the air and produces a second pair of clippers as if from nowhere. He comes at EUGENE from the other side. EUGENE screams. He rushes to the door, but it is locked.]

EUGENE

Isn't this a violation of the fire code?! What if there's a tornado?! Or a fire?! What if I have to pee?!
   [They move in on him, clippers raised.]
Help! Help! Somebody help me! Hey ... what's that over there?

SCHÄFFER

Where?
   [EUGENE darts past them to the window. He tries to lift the latch, but it is stuck.]

SCHÄFFER

There's nowhere to run, Eugene. It's not safe out there.

EUGENE

It's not safe in here!

SCHÄFFER

Here, things are orderly. They follow a certain pattern, a set of rules. It's just a matter of learning the rules, that's all, learning to play along. After a while, you'll become accustomed. You'll begin to anticipate the twists and turns long before they actually occur. Out there, it's utter chaos! You'll be lost! Alone! A ship without a sail!

EUGENE

I don't like your rules!

> *[EUGENE takes one of the giant desks and, with a great effort, hurls it through the window, shattering the glass.]*

You'll never find me! I'll hide from you! I'll live in the shadows! And if you come after me, I'll ... I'll kill you! I'm only trying to protect myself!

> *[EUGENE climbs through the window and disappears. SCHÄFFER goes to the window and stares after him.]*

ROSETTA

You shouldn't have given him the orange.

SCHÄFFER

Return to your—

ROSETTA

> *[Defiantly.]*

What if he tastes of it? What then?

> *[As SCHÄFFER and ROSETTA glare at one another, the buzzing of flies can be heard faintly in the distance. At this sound, SCHÄFFER looks up, startled.]*

SCHÄFFER

What's that sound? What ... what's going on?! I've followed the handbook to the letter!

> [ROSETTA tests the clippers. Lights fade to black.]

* * *

SCENE FOUR:

[Early evening. A public park. The sounds of strange animals howling in the distance, clumping about in the brush. EUGENE sits quivering on a park bench. In his hands, he grips the orange tightly.]

EUGENE
It's all right. They're ... they're probably much smaller than they sound. Tiny little things. Birds. Or ... or insects.
[Howling.]
Insects ... insects often *sound* much ... ahh ... much larger than they really are. It's a ... a kind of ... you know ... defense ... to ... to scare away the ... ahh ... the bigger animals.
[Pause.]
That's it. Insects. I've solved one riddle at least.
[Pause.]
They're ... they're probably terrified, poor things. Huddled in the dark ... all alone ... making as much noise as possible, but ... terrified some bigger insect might come along and call their bluff. It's ... it's certainly good to be a human being capable of defending oneself!
[Howling.]
If ... if not insects, then birds. Birds at the most.
[An enormous roar. The sounds of a kill—a small animal gasping, clawing for its last breath of air.]
Squirrels maybe. Or ... or chipmunks. Perhaps a kitten chasing its first moth. How ... how cute.

*[Enter the VAGRANT. He could be SCHÄFFER's
twin except for the fact that he is much shorter and
covered with a thin layer of filth. His clothes are
tattered and torn. He has no shoes. He hobbles
toward EUGENE, breathlessly, the grinning idiot.
He pauses behind the bench for a moment, then
reaches for the orange. EUGENE screams.]*

Ahh!

VAGRANT
[Jumping back.]

Ahh!

EUGENE
Stay back! Stay back or I'll ... I'll defend myself if I have to! I
can be terribly vicious!
  [The VAGRANT crouches low to the ground.]
Who are you?! What do you want?!
  *[Still crouching low, The VAGRANT spins around
  as if looking for an attacker.]*
What are you ... what are you doing? I'm talking to *you!*

VAGRANT
This one?
  [The VAGRANT points to himself.]

EUGENE
Yes! You!
  [EUGENE glances around nervously.]
Who ... who do you *think* I'm talking to?

VAGRANT

Moon-pie!

EUGENE

What?

VAGRANT

Moon-pie!

EUGENE

Moon-pie?
          [The VAGRANT nods emphatically.]
That ... that's ... what? Your name?
          [The VAGRANT nods—watches EUGENE
          expectantly.]
It's a code-name, isn't it! You're an agent of The Profession!
They've sent you to hunt me down! To drag me back! Well, I ...
I won't go!
          [The VAGRANT does a mad dance, laughing
          wildly.]

VAGRANT

Moon-pie!

EUGENE

I won't go back! Do you hear?! My mind's made up! Are you
listening?! I've had it with The Profession! I'm finished! You
... you might as well just move on to your next ... your next ...
ahh—

VAGRANT

[Clapping wildly.]

Moon-pie! Moonpie!

EUGENE

—victim.

[A beat.]

Oh, you're not one of them. You're just a lunatic. A halfwit.
No offense.

VAGRANT

Fruit-fly!

[EUGENE freezes.]

EUGENE

What was that?

[The VAGRANT waits expectantly.]

What did you say?

VAGRANT

Fruit-fly!

EUGENE

I thought so! Where did you hear that word?!

VAGRANT

This one!

[He points to himself.]

EUGENE

You?

VAGRANT

This one!

EUGENE

You're ... *you're Fruit-fly?*
          [The VAGRANT watches EUGENE expectantly.]
Then you're the one! You're the one behind it all!
          [The VAGRANT does a mad dance, clapping
          wildly.]
But ... you can't be. You're an idiot.

VAGRANT

Moon-pie! Moon-pie!

EUGENE

Oh, you don't even know your own name!
          [EUGENE returns to the bench. The VAGRANT
          follows, sits next to him.]
Are you sure you're not one of them?
          [The VAGRANT grins.]
No ... I guess not. If you were, they'd be here by now. Unless
they sent you to ...
          [EUGENE swallows hard.]
I can't think about that! I won't! It's pointless! Besides, they'll
... they'll never find me here! I'm perfectly safe!
          [The VAGRANT hovers over EUGENE.]
Still, you ... you *do* look familiar.

VAGRANT

The eyes!

EUGENE

[Studying the VAGRANT's eyes.]
Yes ... it is something about the eyes. Or do you mean my eyes
are playing tricks on me?

VAGRANT

The eyes! Darkness! Dream hole!

EUGENE

Oh, well ... that clears it up. Thank you.
   [The VAGRANT makes a dive for EUGENE'S
   orange.]
Hey! Don't touch that! That's my orange! MINE!!!
   [EUGENE wrenches the orange away from the
   VAGRANT.]
Sorry. I'm sorry. I ... I don't mean to be stingy. I'm sure you're
very hungry, but I can't allow you to eat this orange. It's just
that ... well, it's ... it's the key to everything! I know it doesn't
make much sense. I don't understand it quite yet myself. But
one has to have faith, you know, that ... well, that everything will
come clear in the end.
   [Pause.]
It ... it must be nice to be a halfwit. A vagrant, I mean. A
wanderer. You don't have to contemplate. If you're hungry, you
eat. Everything's basic. Primitive. Nothing to confuse the
issue. No one to push you around ... tell you what to do. Maybe
... maybe I should join you!

[EUGENE chuckles. No response from the
VAGRANT.]

Hey ... maybe I *should!* They'd never find me then! And if they
did ... well, they wouldn't recognize me! I'll bet people don't
even give you a second thought, do they?! They probably cross
the street when they see you coming! That's it! That's the
answer! I'll be an outcast! What do you think?

VAGRANT

Hah!

EUGENE

[Defensive.]

What?

[The VAGRANT snorts.]

What's so funny? I ... I could be an outcast!

VAGRANT

Moon-pie! Dreamer's gold!

EUGENE

Why not? I ... I admit I don't have much experience, but I've
always thought of myself as living on the fringes. I'm an outlaw
at heart! Once, when I was five or six ... don't tell anyone, but ...
I once stole a whole handful of comic books from a retarded boy
who lived down the street! Lifted them right under his nose!

[A beat.]

All right, I ... I took them back the next day, but it's the thought
that counts!

[A beat.]

You're not impressed.
> *[A beat.]*

I guess maybe a ... a true outcast only takes what he needs to survive. Is that it? You probably have your own code of conduct. Like the samurai. But I ... I could learn! You could teach me!
> *[The VAGRANT snorts.]*

I think I'd make a respectable outcast!
> *[Pause.]*

All right, what's ... what's wrong with me? Is it the shoes? You're right—shoes might draw attention! Shoes are much too mainstream for me anyway! I've never really liked them! They chafe your feet! Give you blisters!
> *[EUGENE removes his shoes.]*

There!
> *[The VAGRANT stares at EUGENE's feet.]*

I ... I suppose I should get rid of the socks too?
> *[He does.]*

There! You see—I'm willing to make sacrifices. I don't ask for special treatment. I just want to be a regular outcast like everyone else.
> *[The VAGRANT stares hard at EUGENE.]*

What?
> *[EUGENE begins to fidget.]*

What is it? The pants? Just tell me what to do. I'm willing to do whatever it takes. Only I ... I don't have anything else to wear. This is all I've got. I admit, it's a bit dressy for your average outcast, but ... I ... I could dirty it up a bit. A few properly placed smudges, a rip here and there, and you won't recognize it!

[EUGENE attempts to rip his coat.]

This ... ahh ... this is ... good ... good fabric. Maybe if I try the seams.

[He tries the seams—no luck.]

Oh! Wait! I've got it! We could trade! You want to trade?! You know, they say well dressed panhandlers are much more successful! People are more likely to give you a few dollars if you're wearing a coat and tie because they know you must really be in a bind! I ... I know it doesn't make much sense, but it's a proven fact!

[EUGENE begins to take off his clothes.]

Just ... just take off your clothes. I'll even throw in the shoes. And the socks, if you'd like. They're a little smelly, but ...

[The VAGRANT takes EUGENE's shoes. Sniffs them.]

Believe me, you won't be sorry. Those are very expensive shoes! Some kind of fancy leather. My ... my wife, Ibid, bought them for me ...

[EUGENE pauses.]

Ibid ...

[He stares at the pants in his hands for a long moment.]

She ... she has very good taste in ... in clothes.

[Silence. Overcome with sadness, EUGENE sits on the bench. Finally, after a long moment, he offers the VAGRANT his pants.]

Here. Take them.

[He does.]

You want the coat too? Take it! And the tie! Take it all! I don't need it anymore! There! I feel much better now! Free!

So this is what it's like to be an outcast!
>   *[The VAGRANT snorts.]*
What? I ... I still don't qualify? But I've met all the
requirements.

VAGRANT

Hah! Skin-deep!

EUGENE

Well ... I ... I'm sure there are certain spiritual aspects that I'll ...
I'll have to grow into. I mean, I'm sure there are several levels of
vagrancy, and I can't expect to attain the highest levels right
away. These things take time. I'm sure you've been at it for
years, and you want to protect your status by making newcomers
serve a ... a sort of apprenticeship so to speak. And I'm willing
to do that! I'm committed for the long term! But surely I qualify
as at least a Level One outcast! I mean, one has to have some
kind assurance that one is moving in the right direction! After
all, I've given up everything! I've sworn off all material
possessions!

VAGRANT

Not all.

EUGENE

Not all? What ... what do you mean?
>   *[EUGENE clutches the orange tightly.]*
You don't mean *this?* It's not for material reasons that I'm
attached to it! It's what the orange represents! Why can't I be an
outcast with an orange? Where is it written that an outcast can't

own a little piece of fruit?!

  [The VAGRANT holds up his hand—points to it.]

What?

  [The VAGRANT points to his hand.]

Your hand.

  [The VAGRANT nods—pantomimes opening a book.]

Reading. Hand-reading? Braille? Blind?

  [The VAGRANT shakes his head no.]

Book.

  [The VAGRANT nods.]

Hand. Book.

  [Pause. Horrified.]

The *handbook!*

  [The VAGRANT nods emphatically.]

No! Oh, no!

  [The VAGRANT does a mad dance, clapping wildly.]

You're lying! There is no handbook! I refuse to believe it! It's a lie! A fabrication! You just want me to feel I've been left in the dark! Well, I ... I won't have it! Do you hear?! I won't have it! I refuse to cooperate! How do you like that?!

VAGRANT

  [Clapping wildly.]

Refuse!

EUGENE

That's right! Refuse!

VAGRANT

Refuse! Refuse!

EUGENE

Would you ... would you stop that! Stop it! Are you sure I don't
know you?! You remind me of someone! A professor I once—
        [The VAGRANT has worked himself into a frenzy.]
Okay! Okay, I'll make a deal with you! If there really is a
handbook, then show it to me! Show me the handbook, and I'll
believe! I'll follow it to the letter!
        [The VAGRANT stops dancing.]
That's right! Show me! Go on! Do you have it with you?!
        [The VAGRANT nods.]
Well, let's have a look! Where is it?!
        [Pause.]
Go on! I dare you!
        [Long pause.]
See! You can't! You can't show me because it doesn't exist!
There's no such thing!
        [The VAGRANT smiles. Points to his head.]
What?
        [Again, the VAGRANT points to his head.]
Head?
        [Pause.]
It's in your head. You've memorized it.
        [The VAGRANT nods.]
Well ... that doesn't count! I want something solid! I have to see
it with my own two eyes!

VAGRANT

Darkness! Dream hole!

EUGENE

Oh, shut up! Shut up! Just ... just stop babbling for a minute!
[The VAGRANT giggles maniacally.]
I ... I can't think. I'm losing focus. I've ... I've got to–

IBID

[Offstage.]
Eugene!

[EUGENE and the VAGRANT both freeze.]

EUGENE

Did you hear that?! They ... they've found me! They're here!
You! You tipped them off somehow! You sent some kind of
telepathic signal!
*[EUGENE searches desperately for a hiding
place.]*
If you give me away, so help me I'll ... I'll do something awful!
*[EUGENE disappears into a trash can. The
VAGRANT takes a seat on the lid.]*

IBID

[Offstage.]
Eugene! Gene, where are you?!

EUGENE

[From the trash can.]
Ibid? Ibid, is that you?!

IBID

Eugene?!

EUGENE

Ibid!

IBID

Eugene?!

EUGENE

Yes! It's me!

IBID

Where are you?!

EUGENE

Over here!

IBID

Where?!

EUGENE

Here!

[Enter IBID.]

IBID

Where?! I can't see you!

EUGENE

Over here! Inside this trash can!

[IBID approaches the trash can.]

IBID

What are you doing in there?

EUGENE

I was hiding! But now I ... I can't get out!

IBID
[To the VAGRANT who is still seated on the lid.]
Excuse me, but I think my husband's in that can.
[The VAGRANT rises.]
Thank you.
*[The VAGRANT nods and shuffles off, grinning, as
IBID removes the lid. EUGENE pops up.]*
There you are! I've been looking all over.

EUGENE

Are you alone?

IBID

Of course I'm alone. Are you all right? I heard what happened.
[She checks his temperature.]

EUGENE

I'm fine! I ... I escaped with everything intact! How did you
find me?

IBID

Oh ... I have a nose for these things.

EUGENE
[Suspiciously.]
What things?

IBID
Oh ... you know.
[A beat.]
Who's your little friend?

EUGENE
My ... oh ... his name is *Moonpie.*

IBID
Oh, what a nice name! Aren't you going to introduce me?

EUGENE
No. No, I ... I don't think so.

IBID
Why not?

EUGENE
He's a little wacky.

IBID
Oh. Poor thing. That's too bad.

EUGENE
Yes.

IBID

Well ... let's get you home.

EUGENE

No!

IBID

What?

EUGENE

I'm ... I'm not going home. After what's happened, I don't see
how I can. That's the first place they'll look!

IBID

But ... where will you go?

EUGENE

I don't know. I thought I might stay right here. On this bench.

IBID

On this *bench?*

EUGENE

Yes.

IBID

In the *park?*

EUGENE

That's right.

IBID

But ... what about all the wild animals?!

EUGENE

Wild animals?

IBID

That's right! Dinosaurs! And saber-toothed tigers!

EUGENE

Saber ... saber-toothed tigers?
>*[She nods. EUGENE forces a nervous little*
>*laugh.]*

There haven't been any saber-toothed tigers in these parts for millions of years!

IBID

Haven't you heard?

EUGENE

Heard what?

IBID

What happened.

EUGENE

Did something happen?

IBID

They've had a rash of escapes from the tar pits.

VAGRANT

Escape! Escape!

IBID

No one's safe anymore. And after such a long sleep, they're very ... ahh ... *active*. They're eating everything in sight!

EUGENE

Well ... I ... I don't care. I'm staying right here. My mind's made up.

IBID

What about *me?* What am *I* supposed to do?

EUGENE

You can share my bench if you'd like. It's big enough for two.

IBID

It's filthy!

EUGENE

Oh, it's not that bad. Just a little dust.
            [EUGENE wipes a spot off for her.]
There.
            [IBID sits reluctantly.]
You see. Isn't this nice?
            [Pause.]

IBID

I'm not happy here.

                          EUGENE
Why not?

                          IBID
I'm not sure, but I think it has something to do with a fear of
being eaten alive.

                          EUGENE
Don't worry. I'll protect you.

                          IBID
Oh, a fat lot of good you'll do me!

                          EUGENE
It'll be an adventure.

                          IBID
There isn't even a toilet.

                          EUGENE
We'll build one.

                          IBID
How?

                          EUGENE
I don't know! We'll figure it out! We'll live off our wits!

                          IBID
What would people say?! Think of me for once!

EUGENE

I know it sounds a bit unusual, but ... if you really think about it, it's only our perception that's unusual. We've been told there's a certain way to live ... that this is living ... and we ... we never really questioned it. We just sort of went along. But what if it's not the best way? What if there's another way that's better? What if there's something more?!

IBID

But the handbook says—

EUGENE

I don't care what the handbooks says! I can think for myself! And if I want to live in the park and brave the wild animals and steal bread away from little children before they can feed it to the ducks, then ... then that's what I'll do!
        [IBID struggles to hold back the tears.]
Oh, now don't cry.

IBID

They say horrible things happen to people in the park at night! Evil things!

EUGENE

Have you ever stayed in the park after dark? Have you ever seen anything awful happen with your own two eyes?

VAGRANT

Darkness! Dreamhole!

EUGENE
[To the VAGRANT.]

Shut up!

[To IBID.]

Have you?

IBID

Well ... no. But I've heard stories!

EUGENE

How do you know they're true?

IBID

Why wouldn't they be?

EUGENE

Who knows! There could be a million reasons! Who knows
why people say the things they say! Or why they do the things
they do! Who knows what motives they might have! Maybe
they want to keep it all for themselves! Did you ever think of
that?! This place could be the answer to our prayers! It could be
everything we've ever dreamed of!

IBID

Or we could get eaten.

EUGENE

True.

IBID

If we get eaten, what's the point?

EUGENE

Well ... it's a gamble, I admit. But think of the possibilities!

IBID

I don't see them.

EUGENE

You're not trying!

IBID

I am! I really am! I ... I just don't see it the same way you do. I was perfectly content the way things were.

EUGENE

[Explodes.]
Well, I wasn't!!!
[Pause.]
You see this orange? Somewhere inside this ... this mass of ... of pulp and ... and seeds ... and juice ... somewhere inside this skin ... somewhere ... buried ... deep down ... is the answer! The truth! It's my only clue! I can't give that up! I can't condemn myself to darkness!

IBID

What about the children?

EUGENE

Don't start that again!

IBID

We'll have some sooner or later—won't we?

EUGENE

Well ... I ... I guess so. I mean, sure. *Sooner or later.*

IBID

And you'll have to think of their safety too. You won't be able to think only of yourself. You might be able to outwit all of the insects and wild beasts and things, but what about an innocent little baby?

EUGENE

Well, I ... I don't know.

IBID

Come home. We'll pretend like nothing ever happened.

EUGENE

But it did! It *did* happen! For a few minutes, I saw through all the lies! All the deception! The smoke and mirrors! I pulled this orange out of a hat! And even if I can't remember exactly what it means now or ... or put all the ... all the pieces together ... I know that ... that ... *somehow* ... all of this is ... is ... ... all of this is ... ... well, it's ... ... I don't remember what I know, but I know something, and I can't pretend I don't know it!

[EUGENE slumps on the bench. Silence.]

IBID

The sun's almost gone.

EUGENE

There's always the moon.

IBID

No.

EUGENE

No?

IBID

Haven't you heard?

EUGENE

Heard what?

IBID

What happened.

EUGENE

Did something—

IBID

It's fallen out of orbit.

EUGENE

The moon?

IBID

It's headed for Pluto.

EUGENE

I ... I don't understand! How can ... how can *THE MOON* ... I mean ... for God's sake ... WHAT KIND OF WORLD ARE WE LIVING IN?!!!

> *[IBID grabs EUGENE and kisses him passionately—one last desperate kiss. EUGENE is startled by this sudden display of affection, but it calms him somehow. IBID stares into his eyes for a long moment.]*

IBID

I have to go.

EUGENE

What?

IBID

I have to go. The sun's almost gone. I won't stay here after dark.

EUGENE
[Desperately.]

But ... you can't leave *now!* We've almost done it! We're almost free!

IBID

Free? Free from *what?*
       [IBID attempts to contain her mounting rage.]
If you want to throw your life away because ... I don't know ...
because you have a *feeling* ... because some lunatic gave you an
orange ... because the couch is too small ... well ... I can't stop
you. But I won't watch you do it. And I won't put my life in
jeopardy.

EUGENE

Ibid, wait—

IBID

Look at yourself, Eugene! What are you doing?!

EUGENE

I—

IBID

WHAT ARE YOU DOING?!!!
       [EUGENE hesitates.]

EUGENE

I ... I don't know. I don't know what I'm doing exactly. But—

IBID

No "buts!"
     [Pause.]

EUGENE

I think I'm looking for something.

IBID

Something real?

EUGENE

Yes! Something real!

IBID

Something solid? Something that won't change? Something you can count on no matter what kind of craziness goes on around you? An anchor?

EUGENE

Yes! An anchor! That's it exactly!!!

IBID

Then take my hand.

EUGENE

What?

IBID

[Offering her hand.]

Take my hand. I'm your anchor, Eugene. It's not too late. You can still come home. Everything will be just like it was. Just like it's always been. Everything will be forgiven.

EUGENE

But, I ... I don't—

IBID

It doesn't matter what kind of world we live in as long as we have each other!

> *[EUGENE hesitates.]*

Please ... Eugene ... is that orange really more important to you than I am?

> *[They stare at each other in silence. But finally, ever so slowly, EUGENE sets his orange on the bench. He stares at it sadly for a moment—then reaches for IBID's hand.]*

EUGENE

All right.

> *[Just then the VAGRANT snatches the hair from IBID'S head, revealing, beneath the wig, a startled ROSETTA.]*

IBID/ROSETTA

Hey! Give that back! Come here, you little monkey!

EUGENE

What ... what's going on?

ROSETTA

Halfwit!

VAGRANT

Fruit-fly!

EUGENE

I don't—

VAGRANT

Fruit-fly! Fruit-fly!

EUGENE

You're ... you're not Ibid! Where's Ibid?!
> *[ROSETTA lunges for the orange, but EUGENE
> beats her to it.]*

What have you done with my wife?!
> *[ROSETTA removes her apron.]*

ROSETTA

I haven't done anything with her!

EUGENE

I don't understand!

ROSETTA

Oh, for god's sake! Do I have to spell it out for you?!

EUGENE

How am I supposed to know if no one ever—

ROSETTA

There is no Ibid! There never was!

EUGENE

No ... *no Ibid?!*

ROSETTA

That's right! She was a lie! A fabrication!

VAGRANT

The eyes! Darkness! Dreamhole!

EUGENE

But ... why ... why would anyone want to ... ... then ... then she
... you ... you were her and ... and she was ... all along ... there ...
there was never any ...

VAGRANT

Waste of flesh! Tissue! Spit, spit! Irritation!

EUGENE

It doesn't make any sense! It doesn't—

VAGRANT

Redundant organ!

EUGENE

Schäffer!

VAGRANT/SCHÄFFER

Cut off! Eh?!

EUGENE

It *is* you!

SCHÄFFER

Cut off to save the whole! How does it feel?!

EUGENE

I knew it! But you're so ... small. What happened to you? Why, just this morning, you were up to here! A great educator! An integrated member of The Profession! Now look at you! You're melting away! You're ... you're no bigger than *I* am!

ROSETTA

Give me the orange.

EUGENE

What?

ROSETTA

The orange. Give it to me. As a token. Something to carry back to them. A bone—to show I tried.

EUGENE

Never! I'll protect this orange with my life!

ROSETTA

Really? You're willing to give your *life?*

EUGENE

I—

ROSETTA

Fine then.

[To SCHÄFFER.]

You heard him. He's willing to give his life.

SCHÄFFER

Shhh!

*[SCHÄFFER listens intently. There is a faint
humming in the distance.]*

EUGENE

What's he doing?

ROSETTA

Can't you hear them?

EUGENE

Them?

ROSETTA

That faint rustling in the distance ... like leaves ... ashes!

EUGENE

Yes ... yes! I hear it! Just barely!

ROSETTA

They'll be here soon. Then we'll wash our hands of this whole
sordid little mess!

EUGENE

What mess?! What do you mean?! Who are they?! What do
they want?! Please ... I ... when I said I'd give my life, I didn't
actually mean—

SCHÄFFER

Throw yourself! Blindly! Into the fire!

EUGENE

I ... I don't—

SCHÄFFER

The chasm!
                    [The noise in the distance grows louder.]

EUGENE

I don't understand!

ROSETTA

If only you could have forgotten that silly little orange. We
could have carried on the pretense. It was pleasant while it
lasted—wasn't it?

EUGENE

But ... it wasn't real!

ROSETTA
                    [Explodes.]
Who are you to say what's real and what isn't?!

EUGENE

I—

ROSETTA

Did it ever occur to you that maybe I *liked* my little home! My little couch! My little walls! Maybe I *liked* my little life! Did you ever think of that?!

EUGENE

But—

[The humming in the distance grows still louder. The air is filled with the thundering of great hoofs upon the earth. The crashing of trees. EUGENE is terrified.]

What's that?! What's happening?! It's THEM—isn't it?!

ROSETTA

Yes.

EUGENE

I don't understand! What do they want with *me?!*

ROSETTA

With *you?* Hah! It's not *you* they want!

EUGENE

What then?!

[All eyes fall on the orange in EUGENE's hand.]

The orange!

[To SCHÄFFER.]

Here! This belongs to you! I shouldn't have run off with it!
            [EUGENE tosses SCHÄFFER the orange.
            SCHÄFFER, horrified, tosses it back.]
No, really! It's yours! Keep it!
            [Again, EUGENE tosses SCHÄFFER the orange.
            Again, he tosses it back.]
What about you?! You wanted it!
            [EUGENE chases after ROSETTA with the
            orange.]

ROSETTA

Get away from me! It's too late!
            [The three of them play what appears to be a life
            -or-death game of hot potato, frantically tossing
            the orange back and forth until suddenly the stage
            grows dark and they are surrounded by the
            buzzing of a thousand flies.]

ROSETTA

Look at them! Oh! Those dark blue eyes! Those shiny, black
bellies! I've ... I've never seen anything so beautiful in all my
life!

SCHÄFFER

Fruit-fly!
            [SCHÄFFER tosses EUGENE the orange and
            climbs into the trash can.]

EUGENE

Wait! Where are you—

[SCHÄFFER disappears beneath the lid.
EUGENE turns on ROSETTA.]
You! This is all your fault!

ROSETTA

My fault?!

EUGENE

I trusted you! And you ... you've been against me from the start!
If only you'd been honest with me then ... then maybe ... together
... we ... we could have—

ROSETTA

Oh, don't be such a fool!

EUGENE

A fool?! I'm a *fool?!*

ROSETTA

Yes! That's exactly what you are! A great big, silly buffoon!
Always running in circles, asking questions you couldn't
possibly understand! Making funny faces! Come on, Eugene—
be honest. Surely you can see it. You have only one purpose—
to amuse others with your antics, with your pathetic attempts at
comprehension! You're a clown!

EUGENE

A clown?!

ROSETTA

That's right! You have no idea how hard it was to contain myself! Every time you came into the room I wanted to burst out laughing!

[As herself.]
How was your first day?!

[As EUGENE.]
My ... my first day?!

[As herself.]
Your first day! How was it?!

[As EUGENE.]
Ahh ... fine ... fine! It was fine! Just fine! Normal! Just a normal day!

[As herself.]
Are you all right?!

[As EUGENE.]
What?!

[As herself.]
I said, "Are you all right?!"

[As EUGENE.]
Oh! Yes! Fine!

[As herself.]
Is something wrong?!

[As EUGENE.]
No! No! Everything's fine! Just fine! Normal! Why do you ask?!

[As herself.]
You sound a little nervous!

[As EUGENE.]
Me?! No! No! I'm not nervous at all!

[ROSETTA laughs hysterically.]

EUGENE

You think that's funny?!
    [ROSETTA nods through the laughter.]
What about this?! Is this funny?!
    [EUGENE dances around like a monkey.]
Look! I'm a monkey! I'm a dancing bear!
    [EUGENE balances the orange on his nose as he
    dances. ROSETTA laughs even harder.]
You like that?! Huh?! Does that *amuse* you?!
    [ROSETTA is laughing so hard she is near tears.]
What about this?! Is this funny?!
    [Overcome with rage, EUGENE charges at
    ROSETTA and, in one swift motion, forces the
    entire orange into her open mouth. She stumbles
    back, stupefied, clutching her throat—thrashes
    about the stage, unable to breathe, desperately
    trying to dislodge the orange which shows through
    her teeth like a great colored moon. Finally, she
    falls to the ground and, after a few moments, lies
    motionless. The buzzing of the flies fades away.
    Light returns to the stage. Silence. EUGENE
    moves slowly towards ROSETTA. Horrified, he
    shakes her lifeless body.]
My god! What ... what have I done? What have I—
    [He cradles her in his arms, rocking slowly back
    and forth. SCHÄFFER lifts the lid and peeks out
    of his can.]
Ibid? My beautiful Ibid ... I'm sorry! I'm ... I'm sorry! I'll come

home now! I'll come home! We'll pretend like nothing ever ...
nothing ... it didn't ... none of this ... everything will be just like
it was! Ibid? Please? This can't be ... Ibid? This can't ...
somebody ... this isn't happening! This can't be happening! I
just ... I didn't ... oh my god ... what have I ... Ibid?! Somebody
help me! Somebody—
> *[Bells sound. Fireworks.]*

What ... what's going on? I don't understand.
> *[The fireworks continue as SCHÄFFER
> approaches.]*

Did someone get points?

SCHÄFFER
> *[Standing over EUGENE.]*

Yes, Eugene. Someone got points.

EUGENE
Who? Who got points?

SCHÄFFER
Not her.

EUGENE
> *[Still cradling ROSETTA's lifeless body.]*

Not ... not her?

SCHÄFFER
No.
> *[Pause.]*

EUGENE

Then ... who?

[Pause.]

SCHÄFFER

Your progress continues to astound me ... Eugene.

* * *

FADING JOY

Fading Joy premiered at the Asylum Theatre in Las Vegas, Nevada on February 18, 2000, under the direction of Anthony Piersanti. The cast was as follows:

JOY: April Holladay
FAST EDDIE: Bowd Beal

SETTING:
A stretch of beach

SCENE ONE:

[An empty beach. Lots of sand. Waves crashing gently all around. Perhaps an occasional seagull. JOY lies motionless on a lawn chair. She wears a bathing suit, sunglasses, and flip flops. Her face is covered by a big floppy hat. She sighs contentedly. After a few moments, she produces a bottle of tanning lotion and begins spreading it on her arms and legs. Enter FAST EDDIE. He wears a checkered sports coat and a fake moustache which keeps falling off as he hops about madly in the burning sand. He is barefoot.]

FAST EDDIE

Ooh! Ooh! Ooh!
[He approaches JOY, still hopping madly and waving a large suitcase in the air.]
Excuse me! Ooh! Miss!

JOY

Yes?

FAST EDDIE

Do you mind if I—ahh—if I stand in your shadow?!

JOY

What's that?

137

FAST EDDIE

Your shadow!

JOY

My *shadow?*

FAST EDDIE

Yes! Your shadow! My—my feet! The sand!
        *[Still hopping madly, FAST EDDIE points to his
        bare feet.]*

JOY

Oh! Why, certainly. Go right ahead.

FAST EDDIE

Thank you!
        *[He steps into her shadow and lets out a great sigh
        of relief. Then, lowering his suitcase to the
        ground, he takes a good look at JOY for the first
        time. The sight of her seems to trigger something
        in his mind—some half-memory. He pauses and
        studies her carefully.]*

JOY

What are you doing?

FAST EDDIE

Have we met?

JOY

I don't think so.

FAST EDDIE

Are you *sure?*

> *[He stares deep into her eyes. JOY squirms, a bit*
> *unnerved by this inspection.]*

JOY

I ... I don't get many visitors on this beach. I'm sure I'd remember.

FAST EDDIE

It's just that ... there's something about your eyes!

JOY

My eyes?

FAST EDDIE

Yes! The eyes! We've met before!

JOY

Have we?

FAST EDDIE

I'm sure of it!

JOY

But ... you don't seem at all familiar.

FAST EDDIE

Not even a little bit?

> *[He poses, encouraging her to inspect him closely.]*

JOY

No.

FAST EDDIE

How about from this angle?
> *[He poses again.]*

JOY

No.

FAST EDDIE

This one?
> *[He turns his back to her.]*

JOY

I'm sorry.

FAST EDDIE

Hmmm ... I must have been mistaken.
> *[He straightens himself—offers his hand.]*

Fast Eddie.

JOY

What's that?

FAST EDDIE

Fast Eddie. That's the name.

JOY

Oh. What a peculiar name.

FAST EDDIE

Thank you! It was an award!

JOY

An award?

FAST EDDIE

That's right! An award! For selling the most trousers in a single
day!

> *[FAST EDDIE's moustache falls to the ground. He
> replaces it quickly. A disarming little laugh.]*

JOY

What a peculiar sort of award.

FAST EDDIE

Oh, not at all. Why, there's nothing more valuable than a good
name!

JOY

But ... it isn't real.

FAST EDDIE

> *[Fiddling nervously with his moustache.]*

What ... ahh ... *what's* not real?

JOY

The name. It's not really yours.

FAST EDDIE

Oh! The *name!*
  [A great sigh of relief.]
Nevertheless, it's a classic! A real work of art! I have only to
call my name, and people come running from miles around to
buy my wares! Observe!
  [He cups his hands like a megaphone.]
Faaaaaaaaaast EDDIE!
  [They wait. There is no response.]
Faaaaaaaaaaaaaaaast EDDIE!
  [Again, no response.]
We ... we must be out of range.
  *[Again, FAST EDDIE's moustache falls to the
  ground. He pastes it quickly to his lip, then turns
  away and begins to scan the horizon anxiously.]*
You ... you haven't seen any ... ahh ... any very *tall* men, have
you? Abnormally tall? About nine feet?

JOY

Nine feet?

FAST EDDIE

That's right.

JOY

My goodness! No, I haven't seen any men like that.

FAST EDDIE

[Triumphantly.]

Hah! I've lost them!

[He removes the fake moustache.]

JOY

Then again, I haven't really been looking. I mean, they might have passed while my eyes were shut. Or while I was napping.

[Pause. FAST EDDIE pastes the moustache to his lip.]

You're a peculiar sort of fellow ... aren't you?

FAST EDDIE

Peculiar? What ... what do you mean?! In what way peculiar?!

JOY

Well ... you seem a little nervous for one thing, always looking this way or that, constantly fidgeting—

FAST EDDIE

Me? Fidgeting?

[A nervous little laugh.]

Hah! Why not at all! I'm cool as a cucumber! You have to be in this business!

JOY

What business is that?

FAST EDDIE

Sales! Sales is the name of the game! There's no business like sales-business! What business are you in?

JOY

Me? Oh ... I don't have any business.

FAST EDDIE

No business?

JOY

No.

FAST EDDIE

Everybody has some kind of business!

JOY

Not me.

FAST EDDIE

Well ... what do you do?

JOY

Do?

FAST EDDIE

Yes. *Do.* What do you *do?*
    [Pause. She considers this.]
You must do *something* ...

                              JOY
I sit in the sun.

                        FAST EDDIE
Sit in the sun?

                              JOY
That's right.

                        FAST EDDIE
What else?

                              JOY
Nothing.

                        FAST EDDIE
Nothing else?

                              JOY
That's it.

                        FAST EDDIE
Just ... sit in the sun? All day long?

                              JOY
It makes me feel warm and toasty.

                        FAST EDDIE
        [Suddenly, a light-bulb goes off in his head.]
You must get very *thirsty!*

JOY

What?

FAST EDDIE

Thirsty!

[He rummages through his suitcase excitedly.]

JOY

No. Not really.

FAST EDDIE

No?

JOY

I drink from the Ocean.

FAST EDDIE

You can't drink from the Ocean!

JOY

Why not?

FAST EDDIE

It'll make you sick!

JOY

Oh ... really?

FAST EDDIE

It's a proven fact.

JOY

I ... I had no idea.

FAST EDDIE

[Still digging through his suitcase.]

And what do you do at night, when there's no sun to sit in? You must do something then.

JOY

I have long conversations with the moon.

FAST EDDIE

[Finding something in his bag.]

Ah-hah!

[He raises his head.]

Conver ... conversations with the who?

JOY

The moon.

FAST EDDIE

The moon?

JOY

That's right.

[Pause.]

FAST EDDIE

And ... ahh ... what do you talk about? You and ... *the moon.*

JOY

Everything. The meaning of life. The secret of being.

FAST EDDIE

The secret of being?

JOY

That's right. She whispers softly in my ear, and together we wait
for the sun to return.
> *[JOY sighs contentedly.]*

FAST EDDIE

Do you know what you need?
> *[FAST EDDIE pulls a lemonade machine from his
> suitcase and begins to set it up.]*

A lemonade machine!

JOY

A what?

FAST EDDIE

A lemonade machine!

JOY

Oh, no ...

FAST EDDIE

Yes!

JOY

No, I'm perfectly content.

FAST EDDIE

Of course you are! But with a lemonade machine, you'd be even *more* content!

JOY

More content?

FAST EDDIE

That's right!

JOY

How?

FAST EDDIE

Well ... think of it! Everything just as it is now ... but with lemonade!

[Pause—she considers this.]

JOY

No, thank you.

FAST EDDIE

Wait! You don't understand! You see ... if I can only sell 100 of these things ... 100 little lemonade machines ... I'll win a life-saving operation for my baby sister.

JOY

Really?

FAST EDDIE

Yes.

JOY

Your baby sister?

FAST EDDIE

That's right. 200 and my mother can finally have her gall bladder removed. It's been in pieces for years. 1000 and I can buy my beloved Gloria back from those slave traders in the Philippines. She hocked herself to buy me this starter kit.

JOY

That's horrible!

FAST EDDIE

Yes. I know.
        [He tries to look as pathetic as possible.]
How many would you like?

JOY

What?

FAST EDDIE

How many lemonade machines? Five? Ten?

I ... I don'

                    FAST EDDIE
They make fabulous Christmas gifts!

                      JOY
Well, you see, the thing is I ... I don't really like lemonade.

                    FAST EDDIE
Oh, it grows on you!

                      JOY
Does it?

                    FAST EDDIE
Absolutely! You might have to force the first few glasses down,
but after that you won't know how you ever got along without it!

                      JOY
Well ...

                    FAST EDDIE
C'mon! Everybody likes to buy things! It'll make you happy!

                      JOY
I don't have any money.

FAST EDDIE

You don't need money! It's not the money that counts! It's the
sale! The purchase itself! What ... ahh ... what do you have
there? A few dollars?

JOY

No.

FAST EDDIE

A savings bond tucked away somewhere?
          [She shakes her head.]
A promissory note?
          [No.]
A piggy bank then?
          [No again.]
Not even a few pennies?
          [None.]
How about a bowl of soup?
          [She shakes her head sadly.]
Nothing at all?

JOY

Nothing.
          *[Pause. FAST EDDIE's moustache falls to the
          ground.]*

FAST EDDIE

Damn!
          [He replaces it, looks about nervously.]

JOY

Why do you keep doing that?

FAST EDDIE
[Defensive.]

Doing *what?!*

JOY

That.

FAST EDDIE

I'm not doing anything!

JOY

Looking over your shoulder like that and—

FAST EDDIE

Oh, well you ... you have to keep a lookout, you know ... other ...
ahh ... other *salesmen* ... they have no respect for another man's
territory! They'll move in without thinking twice! It's a
dangerous profession! I could tell you stories that would make
your skin crawl! Terrible stories! Why, I've seen the ground
open up and swallow men whole!
[Pause.]
Are ... are you sure you haven't seen any very tall men? Very
tall! Eyes constantly shifting—as if making calculations!

JOY

No. I haven't seen any men like that.
[Pause.]

FAST EDDIE

This machine is the very latest model! The very latest in juicing technology! Twin-carbonated, self-cleaning titanium blades sharp enough to slice a man in half! They were originally developed, you know, by a secret government agency for use in fighter planes! Also ... ahh ... child-proof safety cap.

JOY

It sounds so complicated.

FAST EDDIE

Oh, not at all—a child could operate it!

JOY

But the safety cap ...

FAST EDDIE

That's just for show.
> *[He removes the safety cap and drops it in his pocket.]*

Perhaps you have a friend with some money—a sugar daddy. I don't want to pressure you. I'm only thinking of my sister. Poor thing. She could die at any moment.

JOY

Oh dear.

FAST EDDIE

Yes. I don't want you to feel responsible. Perhaps you could go into business for yourself. Start a lemonade stand, then retire to the Tropics where there's even more sun!

JOY

More sun?

FAST EDDIE

That's right!

JOY

Well ... that might be nice.

FAST EDDIE

There you go! That's the spirit!

JOY

But I still don't have any money.

FAST EDDIE

Give me your flip flops!

JOY

What?

FAST EDDIE

Your flip flops! Quick! Hand them over!

JOY

One little pair of flip flops for a great big lemonade machine?

FAST EDDIE

Yes! Perhaps I can pawn them off somewhere down the line!
    [FAST EDDIE looks over his shoulder nervously.]

JOY

All right. It's a deal.

FAST EDDIE

Sold! To the woman with the dark sunglasses!
    *[JOY hands over her flip flops. FAST EDDIE puts
    them on his feet.]*
Ahh! Much better!

JOY

You know ... I ... I don't think I've ever met anyone quite like
you before.

FAST EDDIE

What do you mean?

JOY

Well, you're so ... driven!

FAST EDDIE

Driven?

JOY
Yes. Driven. It's quite remarkable.
[An awkward pause.]

FAST EDDIE
Well ... I'm off!

JOY
Wait!

FAST EDDIE
What?

JOY
You can't go yet.

FAST EDDIE
Why not?

JOY
You haven't shown me how it works.

FAST EDDIE
Oh. Right. You just ... ahh ... put the stuff in up top there and
then ... then press this little button here ...

JOY
This one?

FAST EDDIE

That's right. And then it ... ahh ... it squirts out lemonade.

JOY

Where do I get the "stuff?"

FAST EDDIE

What stuff?

JOY

The stuff. You said I put "stuff" in up top here.

FAST EDDIE

Oh! The stuff! I almost forgot! I just happen to have a box of
stuff right here!
      [FAST EDDIE pulls a small package from his
      suitcase.]
I ... ahh ... I'm afraid it's extra.

JOY

Extra?

FAST EDDIE

That's right.

JOY

It doesn't come with the machine?

FAST EDDIE

No. It's definitely extra.

JOY

Well, I ... I suppose I could give you these.
          [She offers FAST EDDIE her sunglasses.]

FAST EDDIE

Sunglasses? Hmmm ... might improve my image.
          [He makes the swap.]

JOY

How exciting! My own lemonade machine!

FAST EDDIE

Cups?

JOY

What's that?

FAST EDDIE

Cups? Do you have cups?

JOY

Cups?

FAST EDDIE

That's right. Cups.

JOY

No. Are they extra too?

FAST EDDIE

I'm afraid so.
          [Pause.]

JOY

I'll just use my hands.

FAST EDDIE

Suit yourself. I'm off then. Have to stay on top of the game! So
much to sell, and so little time to sell it!

JOY

Wait!

FAST EDDIE

What now?
          [Pause. She hesitates.]
What? What is it?

JOY

Would ... would you ...

FAST EDDIE

What?! What?! Spit it out! I haven't got all day!

JOY

Would you like some lemonade?

FAST EDDIE

No thanks. I never touch the stuff.

JOY

Oh.

FAST EDDIE

I'm sorry. I don't mean to be rude, it's just that ... well, I have to
get back on the road. I have a quota to meet—

JOY

I understand.

FAST EDDIE

Well ... goodbye then.

JOY

Goodbye then.
                    [He turns to go.]
Goodbye.

FAST EDDIE

Goodbye.

JOY

Good luck.

FAST EDDIE

Thank you.
                [He turns to go.]

JOY

Have you ... I'm sorry, I ... I just ... I know this isn't any of my business, but I was thinking. Have you ever thought of setting up shop somewhere?

FAST EDDIE

Setting up shop?

JOY

Yes!

FAST EDDIE

No ... never thought of that.

JOY

Right here on this beach for instance!

FAST EDDIE
            [Skeptical.]
Here?

JOY

Yes! It's the perfect spot! Lots of sunshine—people are bound to get thirsty! You could put up a little stand!
            [FAST EDDIE considers this.]

FAST EDDIE

A lemonade-stand stand.
            [Pause.]
Interesting.

JOY

That's right. And you could make a little sign. Or a billboard!

FAST EDDIE

A billboard! Magnificent!

JOY

And there's no one else in sight! You'd have a monopoly!

FAST EDDIE

It sounds too good to be true!

JOY

Plus you wouldn't burn your feet walking in the hot sand all the time.

FAST EDDIE

My god ... you're a visionary!

JOY

You'll have your quota met in no time. You can get your beloved out of hock. Settle down. Start a family.

FAST EDDIE

Yes, but ... if the tall men should happen by ... I'd be a sitting duck.

JOY

Well ... in that case, I could cover for you until they pass. You duck down behind the counter, and I claim ownership until

they're out of sight. Who knows—they might even buy
something!

FAST EDDIE
[Suddenly very serious.]
No! No, you don't want to deal with these people! Believe me!
They're a dangerous lot! All of them! You have no idea what
they're capable of!

JOY
Well ... all right, then. I'll ... I'll tell them we're temporarily
closed for repairs.
        [Pause. He considers this.]

FAST EDDIE
You know ... it just might work.

JOY
Then you'll do it?

FAST EDDIE
Yes. I'll do it. I'll set up shop!

JOY
Oh! Good!

FAST EDDIE
You know, I think this may be just what I've been missing.
Something permanent. Something solid. A stand! Something
you can look at and feel a real sense of accomplishment!

JOY

Is there anything I can do to help?

FAST EDDIE

Oh, no. No, this is real *man's* work, you know, building things,
working with your hands. Nails, hammers, saws. You just sit
there and enjoy your sun. Have some lemonade. Or ... oh! I
know! You could gather some wood!

JOY

Wood?

FAST EDDIE

That's right. Lumber. To build the stand.

JOY

You need *wood?*

FAST EDDIE

Yes.

JOY

Oh.
        [Pause.]
I ... I don't have any wood.

FAST EDDIE

No wood?
        [Pause.]
That puts a kink in the plan—doesn't it?

[Pause.]
Well, it was a pipedream anyway!
          [FAST EDDIE begins to pack his things.]

JOY

Wait! We ... we could tear down my chair.

FAST EDDIE

Yes!
          [Pause. They exchange a glance.]
I mean ... *no* ... no, we couldn't do that.

JOY

Why not?

FAST EDDIE

Well ... it's your chair.

JOY

I don't mind.

FAST EDDIE

It wouldn't be right. I don't want to take your chair.

JOY

Please—take it. It's my chair. I want you to have it.

FAST EDDIE

I don't want your chair. There must be some wood around here
somewhere. Driftwood maybe.

JOY

You can pay me back later.

FAST EDDIE

I don't like to borrow on credit.

JOY

You can buy me a new one after you've built your empire.

FAST EDDIE

My ... my *empire?*

JOY

That's right.

FAST EDDIE

You ... you really think I could build an empire?

JOY

Why not?

[Pause. He considers this.]

FAST EDDIE

You know ... you're right! Why not?! Why shouldn't I build an empire! Other people build empires! Why shouldn't I?!

JOY

That's the spirit!

FAST EDDIE

All right! It's a deal! I'll take your chair—but I'm going to buy you a new one as soon as my ship comes in! First thing on the list!

> [He takes the chair.]

Now ...

> [He contorts the chair, twists it, turns it on its end trying to fashion some kind of stand.]

JOY

Is she beautiful—your beloved?

FAST EDDIE

What's that?

JOY

Your beloved. Is she very pretty?

FAST EDDIE

Oh, the prettiest. That's why they wanted her for the slave trade.
> [Still fiddling with the chair.]

This may take some work.

JOY

Did you love her very much?

FAST EDDIE

Hmmm?

JOY

Did you love her?

FAST EDDIE

Oh. More than anything.

JOY

Did you bring her flowers?

FAST EDDIE

Of course.

JOY

And candy?

FAST EDDIE

Sometimes.

JOY

Did you write her poems?

FAST EDDIE

Poems?

JOY

That's right. Poems. Or love songs!
        [FAST EDDIE considers this.]

FAST EDDIE

I ... I'm not sure. I mean, I'm sure I did. I must have.

[Pause.]
I don't really remember.

JOY

You don't *remember?*

FAST EDDIE

Well ... it's been such a long time. After a while, things begin to
get fuzzy, you know.

JOY

But ... how could you forget something like that?

FAST EDDIE

If you want to know the truth ... I ... well ... I can hardly
remember her face anymore. I try. I try to picture her just as she
boarded that slave ship. The Filipino captain glaring at her
lustfully. She wore a blue dress I'd bought for her—a frilly thing
with lots of lace ... or ... or maybe it was green ... no blue ...
definitely blue ... but there wasn't any lace ... was there lace? I
think there was. Wait ... did she wear a dress? Maybe it wasn't
a dress at all. Maybe it was a pantsuit. I really can't be sure.
Anyway, at the last moment, she turned back and smiled as if to
say, "Don't worry. We're bound together, you and I. Someday
soon, we'll be together again." And I knew—I knew she was
right! She was the most beautiful thing I had ever seen in all my
life! So innocent! So pure! All I wanted was to have her back
again. To protect her. To take her someplace far away from that
awful ship. But it was too late. He yanked her away. And now
... when I try to picture her face ... there's ... there's always

something wrong ... something out of place. I'm not sure what ...
the nose ... the mouth ... the eyes ... I ... I don't know ... I can't
put a finger on it ... but it's never quite her.

JOY

That's horrible!

FAST EDDIE

I know.

JOY

If someone sacrificed themself for me like that I ... I could never
forget them! Ever! No matter what happened! I'd remember
them for all eternity!

FAST EDDIE
[Still fiddling with the chair.]
Damn this thing!

JOY

Here—let me.
          *[JOY takes the chair and turns it on its side. She
          sets FAST EDDIE's bag on top.]*
There. A stand.
          [FAST EDDIE examines her construction.]

FAST EDDIE

Well ... it's ... it's kind of *crude* ... but I guess it'll do.

JOY

I didn't mean to upset you. I'm sure it's not your fault that you can't remember. I mean, I'm sure there's a perfectly good explanation. Maybe ... maybe it just wasn't meant to be. Maybe she wasn't your true love.

[Pause.]

Would you do my back?

FAST EDDIE

Excuse me?

JOY

My back.

[She produces a bottle of suntan lotion.]

FAST EDDIE

Oh. Certainly.

[He begins to apply lotion to her back.]

JOY

Lower.

[He complies.]

All the way down.

FAST EDDIE

How's that?

JOY

You have strong hands.

FAST EDDIE

Do I?

JOY

Yes.
[Pause.]
I suppose you must be very experienced.

FAST EDDIE

What do you mean?

JOY

Well ... I suppose you've seen the world.

FAST EDDIE

Bits and pieces.

JOY

I haven't seen anything.

FAST EDDIE

Nothing?

JOY

No. Just this beach.

FAST EDDIE

Well ... this is a very nice beach.

JOY

I thought so! I mean, I ... I thought it must be.

FAST EDDIE

But it must get lonely sometimes. I mean, a beautiful young
woman like yourself ... all alone ... with only the sun and moon
to keep you company.

JOY

Yes. It does. It does get lonely.
        [FAST EDDIE inches closer.]

FAST EDDIE

Does it?
        [She nods. He kisses her. She pulls away.]
What's wrong?

JOY

I ... I've never been kissed before.

FAST EDDIE

Never?
        [She shakes her head.]
I'm sorry. I didn't mean to—

JOY

Do it again.

FAST EDDIE

Are you sure?

                         JOY

Yes!

                    FAST EDDIE

All right.
                    [He kisses her.]
Well ... what do you think?
                    [Pause.]

                         JOY

I suppose you've kissed a lot of girls.

                    FAST EDDIE

A few.
                         JOY
Do they always fall at your feet?

                    FAST EDDIE

Sometimes.

                         JOY

Do you want me to fall at your feet?

                    FAST EDDIE

If you'd like.

                         JOY

I don't know what I'd like. It's all very confusing. A few
moments ago, I was perfectly content to just sit in my chair and
soak up the sun. Then you come along, and ... suddenly

everything's different! It's all so complicated! I feel as if the ground is shifting beneath my feet!

FAST EDDIE

It's not so complicated really.

JOY

No?

FAST EDDIE

No. It's all very natural.
> *[He slides a hand around her waist.]*

JOY

So ... what happens next?

FAST EDDIE

Well ...
> *[He begins to kiss her neck.]*

JOY

Our empire. What's the next step?

FAST EDDIE
> *[Taken aback.]*

Our empire?!

JOY

I've never built an empire before. I don't know what to do. Give me a task.

FAST EDDIE

What do you mean *our* empire?

JOY

Well, it *is* my chair.

FAST EDDIE

Whoa!

JOY

What?

FAST EDDIE

Whoa! You *gave* me the chair!

JOY

Right.

FAST EDDIE

The chair belongs to me now! It's my chair!

JOY

You promised to pay me back.

FAST EDDIE

I *will!* I *will* pay you back! But—

JOY

Well, until then I have a certain interest in the success of your lemonade-stand stand—don't I?

[Pause.]
I just want to help.

                              FAST EDDIE
Well ... all right. I suppose there's no harm in that. You can be
my assistant.

                              JOY
Your assistant?! Really?!

                              FAST EDDIE
That's right.

                              JOY
What would my duties be?! I mean, what exactly would I *do*—
as your assistant?

                              FAST EDDIE
Well ... you could ... ahh ... you could be in charge of
advertising.

                              JOY
Advertising?

                              FAST EDDIE
That's right. You provide the customers. I provide the
lemonade.

JOY
[Hardly able to contain her enthusiasm.]
The customers! Oh! I want lots of customers!

FAST EDDIE
So do I. The more, the merrier.

JOY
I'm glad we agree! I think we should get started right away!

FAST EDDIE
All right.

JOY
What would you prefer—girls or boys?

FAST EDDIE
Huh?

JOY
You're right! What does it matter?! We'll have all kinds!

FAST EDDIE
Exactly.

JOY
But wouldn't it be nice to start with a little girl?

FAST EDDIE
What are you talking about?

JOY
I've always liked the name "Emmanuella." What do you think?

FAST EDDIE
Won't they come with names?

JOY
No, I think you have to name them. What if it's a boy? How would you feel about "Eddie Jr?"

FAST EDDIE
Now wait just a minute!

JOY
You're right. He should have his own name. We don't want him to spend his whole life trying to live up to your image. How about "Jack?"

FAST EDDIE
Are you suggesting that we ... *make* customers.

JOY
Well—how else? This beach isn't exactly teeming with life.

FAST EDDIE
I think it might be more financially viable to find customers we don't have to feed and clothe!

JOY

Yes, but think about it—they'll be customers for life! They'll be entirely dependant on us!

FAST EDDIE

That's what I'm afraid of! Look—I'm sure an attractive young woman like yourself can find *some* other way to entice customers towards our little stand.

JOY

What do you mean?

FAST EDDIE

Well ... you know ... I ... I don't ... look, this is a new operation. We'll have to sort of feel things out ... you know. Experiment.

JOY

Why do we have to experiment?

FAST EDDIE

Well ... for instance ... in your case ... to determine how best to utilize ... one's ... ahh ... one's *assets* ... or ... or rather ... to focus ... yes ... to focus one's ... one's advertising ... you know ... campaign ... to ... ahh ... to ... to one's best advantage.

JOY

You want me to utilize my assets?

FAST EDDIE

Yes.

JOY

How?

FAST EDDIE

Well ... off the top of my head ... and I'm just brainstorming here ... I'd say you should make sure to display them—your *assets*—in a prominent position, so as to attract as much attention as possible.

JOY

I'm not sure I understand.

FAST EDDIE

Well—

JOY

Aren't they displayed *now*—my assets?

FAST EDDIE

Yes ... yes, they are ... but you could display them more *prominently*.

JOY

More prominently?

FAST EDDIE

That's right.

JOY

What does that mean?

FAST EDDIE

Look—

JOY

You're not suggesting that I take off my—

FAST EDDIE

No! No! That's not what I'm suggesting at all! But it's a
brilliant idea! I'm glad you thought of it! We can get you a little
stool and put it—

JOY

Shame on you!

FAST EDDIE

What—I'm only thinking of the business!

JOY

What would the children think?! I mean, the customers!

FAST EDDIE

Ah-hah!

JOY

What?

FAST EDDIE

You said children!

JOY

I meant customers.

FAST EDDIE

But you *said* children!

JOY

Don't change the subject! You want me to take off my clothes!

FAST EDDIE

That's completely beside the point!

JOY

Is it?!

FAST EDDIE

Yes! Because you're trying to manipulate me into some sort of weird domestic relationship!

JOY

I'm trying to manipulate *you?!*

FAST EDDIE

That's right!

JOY

Okay, who showed up on whose beach pushing lemonade machines like it was the end of the world and talking about "The eyes! The eyes! We've met before!"

FAST EDDIE

Oh, give me a break! Everybody's selling something! Buying and selling, that's what it's all about! It's obvious what I'm selling! What I want to know is—what are *you* selling, lady! What load of crap are you trying to push off on *me?!*

JOY

I'm not pushing any load of crap!

FAST EDDIE

No?! What assurances do I have?! I don't know anything about you—do I? You haven't told me anything about yourself! Why is that?! I don't even know your name!

JOY

Joy! My name is Joy! You're so self-centered you never even asked!

FAST EDDIE

And where are you from, *Joy?*

JOY

Where am I *from?*

FAST EDDIE

That's right! Where are you *from?!* What is your *purpose* here on this beach?!

JOY

It's ... it's none of your business!

FAST EDDIE

What are you trying to hide?!

JOY

Nothing! I'm not trying to hide anything! I ... I don't *remember* where I'm from! I don't *know* my purpose!

FAST EDDIE

Hah! What are you trying to pull?! Are you working for *them?!*

JOY

Them?

FAST EDDIE

Them! The tall men!
          [Pause. FAST EDDIE recoils from her in horror.]
You are! You *are!* My god! You're trying to stall me until they arrive!

JOY

Why are you so afraid of these tall men?

FAST EDDIE

I'm not afraid!

JOY

Then why are you always looking over your shoulder, and ... and why are you wearing that stupid fake moustache?!

FAST EDDIE
THIS IS NOT A FAKE MOUSTACHE!!!
   [His moustache falls to the ground.]
Damn!

JOY

I hope they catch you! The tall men! I hope they catch you and
... and cut off your head! I hope they tear out your liver and feed
it to the fish! You probably deserve it! You're not a nice
person! You've probably done something awful! Something
unspeakably cruel! I'm going to close my eyes, and when I open
them I don't want to see you anymore!

FAST EDDIE

Fine!

JOY

Fine!

FAST EDDIE

I'll set up shop someplace else!

JOY

Someplace far away I hope!

FAST EDDIE

Don't worry!

JOY

I'm closing my eyes!

FAST EDDIE

Good! Close them! You won't see me again!

JOY

I hope not!

FAST EDDIE

Goodbye!

JOY

Goodbye!

  [Exit FAST EDDIE.]

Wait!

  [She opens her eyes, but he is gone.]

* * *

SCENE TWO:

[*The beach. It is darker now. JOY sits shivering in her lawn chair. She stares up at the moon.*]

JOY

Hello? Mother Moon? It's me. Joy. Can you hear me?
  [*Pause.*]
Hello?
  [*Pause.*]
I know you're up there. I can see you, but ... you're so far away. Why are you so far away?
  [*Pause.*]
I just want to talk for a few minutes. Like we used to. Do you remember how we used to talk? It was such fun! What ... what was it we used to talk about? I've forgotten. Beautiful things, I ... I know that, but ... I can't ... I can't quite ...
  [*Pause.*]
I don't even remember how I got here. Isn't that strange? I know I came from someplace warm. Warm and dark. And water. There was water. I remember floating in the night sky ... or ... or deep in the ocean. And I remember voices. Big soft angel voices. They told me things. Secrets. They sang to me. Beautiful songs! About ...
  [*Pause.*]
I ... I can't remember what they were about anymore. I try, but ... they're gone. Won't you tell me, Mother Moon? Won't you whisper in my ear just one more time? Please?
  [*Pause.*]

189

Why won't you answer me?
> *[Pause.]*

What have I done wrong?
> *[Silence. Enter FAST EDDIE. His clothes are tattered and torn. Once again, he is barefoot. The flip-flops are nowhere to be found—nor are the sunglasses. His fake moustache, too, has disappeared. He trudges past JOY, dully, in a kind of daze.]*

Hey! Hey! Wait! Fast Eddie!
> *[FAST EDDIE pauses.]*

FAST EDDIE

Who?

JOY

Fast Eddie!

FAST EDDIE

I'm sorry ... you've mistaken me for someone else.

JOY

No! It's you! I remember!

FAST EDDIE

I don't know any Fast Eddie.

JOY

What's your name then?!

FAST EDDIE

Eddie.

JOY

You see!

EDDIE
[Sadly.]
No. *Just* Eddie. Nothing more. Just plain Eddie.

JOY

Look, either way, you sold me this machine!

EDDIE

Did I?

JOY

Yes! You did! Don't try to worm your way out of it!

EDDIE

I don't deny the possibility that I may have sold you that
machine. But you can't expect me to remember every customer
I've dealt with over the years.

JOY

As a dealer of lemonade machines, you have certain
responsibilities!

EDDIE

Do you have the warranty?

JOY

You didn't offer a warranty!

EDDIE

I always offer a warranty.

JOY

Well, you didn't this time! Look, I need more "stuff"—you know, to make the lemonade. I'm all out. I ... I don't have much left to offer, but ...

EDDIE

There *is* no more.

JOY

What?

EDDIE

There's no more stuff.

JOY

No more stuff?

EDDIE

That's right.

JOY

But ... how can that *be?!*

                              EDDIE
They've taken it off the market.

                              JOY
Off the market?! *Stuff?!*

                              EDDIE
That's right.

                              JOY
Why?!

                              EDDIE
It wasn't selling.

                              JOY
Then ... then my lemonade machine is useless.

                              EDDIE
I'm afraid so.
                    [Pause.]

                              JOY
I want my sunglasses back.

                              EDDIE
What?

                              JOY
My sunglasses! Hand them over!

EDDIE

I can't.

JOY

Why not?!

EDDIE

They've been stolen.

JOY

Oh ...

EDDIE

I'm sorry.

JOY

The flip flops then!

EDDIE

Gone.

JOY

Gone?

EDDIE

That's right.

JOY

The flip flops too?!

EDDIE

Yes. Along with all of my awards. Every last one. At first I
made good time in the flip-flops, but after a while I got
complacent, and they overtook me.

JOY

The tall men?

EDDIE

That's right. They beat me within an inch of my life. Left me
for dead. I've nothing left. Not even my name.

JOY

Oh ... you poor thing. You were so proud of that name.

EDDIE

Yes. It really was something—wasn't it?

JOY

That's so unfair. That name couldn't possibly have meant
anything to anyone but you.

EDDIE

Oh, it's not the goods that matter. It's the theft itself. That's
what counts.
        [Pause.]
I remember you now.

JOY

[Hopeful.]
Do you? Really?

EDDIE

Yes. You wanted to move to the Tropics. More sun.
[Pause.]
Why didn't you go?

JOY

Oh. Well ... when people wanted lemonade, I forgot to charge
them until it was too late. And then ... you know ... I ... I didn't
want to make a big fuss. I didn't want to disappoint anybody.

EDDIE

Well ... you still have the sun. That's more than I can say.

JOY

No.

EDDIE

No?

JOY

It's not the same anymore.

EDDIE

Not the same—the sun?

JOY

It's so bright. It hurts my eyes. And the sand burns my feet. My hands are all sticky from the lemonade. And there's no one to talk to.

EDDIE

What about the moon?

JOY

I've forgotten her language. Besides ... I ... I was a child back then. It's just not the same.

EDDIE

Oh ... that's too bad.

JOY

Yes.
          [Pause.]
Did your sister ever have that operation?

EDDIE

What sister?

JOY

Your—

EDDIE

Oh. No. No ... she didn't.

JOY

I'm so sorry.
> *[He nods sadly.]*

What about your mother?

EDDIE

Dead.

JOY

And your beloved?

EDDIE

I only sold 99 machines. It didn't even cover my expenses. 100 was the magic number.

JOY

How tragic. You must miss her terribly—your beloved.

EDDIE

Yes. Although, to be perfectly honest ... I'm not sure if she ever existed.

JOY

What do you mean?

EDDIE

Well, I can't seem to remember if she was ever really real or ... or just a dream ... a phantom ... something I made up to get me through the day.

JOY

You made her up?!

EDDIE

It's possible. I can't be sure. It was such a long time ago.
Sometimes I'm almost certain she was real ... and sometimes ...
well ...
    [Pause.]

JOY

Wouldn't it be sad if she *was* real? If she *was* real ... and you'd
just ... forgotten her ... wiped her accidentally from your mind ...
lost her in there somewhere ... forever ... like a ring that's fallen
into the bushes ... someone that close to you ... wouldn't that be
sad?

EDDIE

Yes. It would.
    [Pause.]

JOY

What if ... what if we're *all* like that?

EDDIE

Like what?

JOY

Like ... like ghosts ... in someone's mind ... gradually fading ...
fading ... until finally ... one day ... we just disappear ... drift into
nothingness. Wouldn't that be sad?

EDDIE

Are you sure we've never met before?

JOY

Of course we've met—when you sold me the machine.

EDDIE

What machine?

JOY

The lemonade machine.

EDDIE

Ah! The lemonade machine! Now that brings back memories! Yes, sir! Those were the days! Traveling from one town to the next with nothing but the shirt on your back and a case full of ... ahh ... a case full of ... ... what ... what was it again?

JOY

What was what?

EDDIE

What I sold.

JOY

Lemonade machines.

EDDIE

Lemonade machines! That's right! Those were the days!

JOY
[Concerned.]
Are you all right?

EDDIE

I'm fine.

JOY

I mean ... are you *okay?* You seem a little ... I don't know,
confused.

EDDIE

Confused?
[Laughs.]
Why, not at all! My mind's sharp as a tack! It has to be in this
business, you know.

JOY
[Testing him.]
What business?

EDDIE

I have no idea.

JOY

I think there's something wrong with you.

EDDIE

Wrong? In what way?

JOY

Did you hit your head?

EDDIE

I don't think so. But then, if I *had*, and it caused some sort of
amnesia, I might not *remember* hitting my head.

JOY

You don't have any bumps or bruises.
        [She feels his forehead.]
You do have a bit of a fever though.

EDDIE

Do I?

JOY

Maybe you should lie down.

EDDIE

Oh, I don't think that's necessary ... unless you want to join me?

JOY

It doesn't concern you at all—the fact that you can't remember
anything?

EDDIE
        [Laughs.]
Why, not at all! My mind's sharp as a tack! It has to be in this
business, you know.

JOY
[Testing him.]
What business?

EDDIE

Ahh ...

JOY

There! You see!

EDDIE

See what?

JOY

Does any of this seem at all familiar to you—this conversation?
Even a little bit?

EDDIE

No.

JOY

Something really is wrong. You poor thing. I hope it's not
contagious. Ask me something about myself.

EDDIE

Where are you from?
[Pause. JOY puts a hand to her mouth, horrified.]
What's wrong?

JOY

I've caught your disease!

EDDIE

I have a disease?!

JOY

Yes! Well ... maybe.

EDDIE

What do you mean—*maybe?* Do I or don't I?! Give it to me straight!

JOY

Well, I ... I don't know–

EDDIE

You don't *know?!* What kind of doctor are you?!

JOY

I'm not a doctor at all. I'm just a girl.

EDDIE

Well, then what business do you have diagnosing me?! You should be ashamed of yourself! You scared me half to death!

JOY

I ... I'm not trying to *diagnose* you. It's just that ... well, you seem very confused, and I—

                                EDDIE
Confused about what?

                                JOY
Well, the lemonade machines, for instance.

                                EDDIE
What lemonade machines?

                                JOY
The ones you used to sell.

                                EDDIE
See—you're the one that's confused. I never sold lemonade
machines.

                                JOY
Of course you did. I have one right here. See?
            [She shows him the lemonade machine.]

                                EDDIE
Is that what that is?
            [JOY nods.]
But ... I don't even like lemonade.

                                JOY
Oh! It grows on you!

                                EDDIE
Does it?

JOY

Yes! You may have to force down the first few glasses, but after that ... Don't you remember? We were going to build an empire!

EDDIE

An *empire? Really?*

JOY

Yes.

EDDIE

You and me?

JOY

That's right.

EDDIE

How far did we get?

JOY

Not far.
          [Pause.]
We built a stand.

EDDIE

A stand? Really? Now that's a real accomplishment! That's something to be proud of! Yes, sir—a stand!
          [Pause. JOY studies him carefully.]
What are you doing?

JOY
You look ... different somehow.

EDDIE
Do I?

JOY
Yes.
[She studies him.]
Didn't you ... Did you used to wear a moustache?

EDDIE
A moustache?

JOY
Yes. A long time ago.

EDDIE
Did I?

JOY
That's what I'm asking.

EDDIE
I don't recall.

JOY
Was it you or someone else?

EDDIE

It might have been me. I can't be sure.

JOY

I seem to recall a moustache.

EDDIE

Yes ... I seem to recall a moustache as well!
[They consider this.]
Was it my father?

JOY

What?

EDDIE

My father—was it my father who wore the moustache?

JOY

I don't know your father. Do I?

EDDIE

Did my father wear a moustache?

JOY

Do I know your father?

EDDIE

I don't know. You might.

JOY

I don't remember him.

EDDIE

I hardly remember him myself.

JOY

That's awful!

EDDIE

What's awful?

JOY

That you don't remember him.

EDDIE

Remember who?

JOY

What?

EDDIE

Who?

JOY

Who what?

[Pause.]

EDDIE

I'm sorry. I seem to be a bit confused. What were we just talking about?

JOY

I'm not sure. Someone. Or ... something. A ring, I think! A ring in the bushes!

EDDIE

There are no bushes here.

JOY

No.

[Long pause. JOY seems disturbed.]

EDDIE

It couldn't have been very important.

JOY

No.

[Pause.]

EDDIE

If it was important, we'd remember.

JOY

Yes.

[Pause.]

I ... I think something's wrong. I'm not sure what, but ... I have this feeling that—

                    EDDIE
Do you mind if I ask a question?

                    JOY
Go ahead.

                    EDDIE
How did we get here?

                    JOY
What?

                    EDDIE
Here. In this place. How did we—

                    JOY
I don't know.

                    EDDIE
That's strange. Neither do I.

                    JOY
Where are we?

                    EDDIE
I don't know. A beach somewhere.

                    JOY
Can I swim?

EDDIE

If you'd like.

JOY

No, no—have I ever *learned? To swim?*

EDDIE

I don't know. Have you?

JOY

I don't know.

EDDIE

Perhaps you should give it a try.

JOY

What—just jump in?

EDDIE

That's right.

JOY

What if I drown?!

EDDIE

I'll save you.

JOY

Have *you* learned?

                              EDDIE
What?

                              JOY
To swim.

                              EDDIE
I don't know. Have I?

                              JOY
I have no idea.
            [Pause.]

                              EDDIE
Perhaps we should stay here. On this chair.

                              JOY
All right.

                              EDDIE
Just to be safe.
            [Silence.]

                              JOY
Do you mind if I ask a question?

                              EDDIE
Go ahead.

JOY

Whose chair is this?

EDDIE

What?

JOY

This chair. This chair. Whose chair is this?

EDDIE

Isn't it yours?

JOY

I don't think so. It doesn't look familiar.

EDDIE

It must be someone else's.

JOY

What a strange and unfamiliar chair!

EDDIE

It is strange and unfamiliar.

JOY

It frightens me.

EDDIE

Don't be frightened. It's only because it's unfamiliar that it
frightens you. It's only a matter of time before you grow

accustomed to it. Eventually, you might find it comforting. You might even come to think of it as your own.

JOY

Do you think so?

EDDIE

Yes.

JOY

But it must belong to someone.
[A disturbing thought.]
What if they come for it? What if the owner of the chair returns?

EDDIE

We'll have to give it to them, I suppose.

JOY

But we'll have nothing to sit on.

EDDIE

If only this was *our* chair. Wouldn't that be nice?

JOY

Our own chair. Yes. That would be nice.
[Pause.]

EDDIE

Do you mind if I ask a question?

JOY

Go ahead.

EDDIE

Who are you?

JOY

I ... I'm not sure. Don't you know me?

EDDIE

No.

JOY

No?

EDDIE

Do *you* know *me?*

JOY

I don't think so.

EDDIE

I wonder what we're doing here.
 [Pause.]
Perhaps we've come to collect seashells. Although, if that's the case, we haven't been very successful, have we?
 [Pause.]
Perhaps we've come to collect seashells, and we've only just arrived! That would explain not only what we're doing here, but the lack of seashells as well.

[Pause.]
Although, if we *had* come to collect seashells, we would probably have, at the very least, some sort of bag or sack, something to carry the loot so to speak.

[Pause.]
Perhaps we've come to collect seashells, we've only just arrived, and we've forgotten our bag! That would explain not only what we're doing here, but the lack of seashells as well as the absence of a bag.

[Pause.]
Although ... if that were the case, we would probably have returned home once we realized that we'd forgotten our bag.

[Pause.]
Perhaps we haven't come to collect seashells at all! Perhaps we've been put here by someone else, planted in this spot for some unknown purpose. Perhaps we're employees of some sort. Watchmen. Hired guns to frighten away any trespassers that might wander onto this beach.

[Pause.]
Although, if we *were* watchmen, we'd probably have some sort of weapon, a means of defending oneself, a gun or, at the very least, a large stick.

[Pause.]
Perhaps we're trespassers ourselves! Perhaps we're up to no good! Perhaps we've come here for some dark purpose of our own! To do some evil to the owner of this beach! Of course, that's assuming not only that there *is* an owner, but that he's done us some injustice ...

[Pause.]
I know! What if the owner is an old friend! Perhaps we'd made

arrangements to meet him here only ... only he can't come because he's passed away ... silently ... in the night. Or perhaps he's lost his mind ... simply forgotten we're here ... but we, not knowing, continue to wait, unaware that—

> *[EDDIE notices that JOY has wandered off to the water's edge.]*

What are you doing?

JOY

It's so dark. The water. It's so ... *dark.*

EDDIE

It is dark.

> *[Pause.]*

JOY

Hold my hand.

EDDIE

What?

JOY

Hold my hand. I'm frightened.

EDDIE

But ... I hardly know you.

JOY

I don't care! I'm frightened, and I want you to hold my hand!

EDDIE
All right. What are you frightened of?

JOY
I don't know!

EDDIE
Well, you must have *some* idea.

JOY
I ... I'm afraid I might disappear.

EDDIE
      [Laughs.]
Disappear?

JOY
That's right.

EDDIE
What—what do you mean? Just vanish?

JOY
Yes.

EDDIE
Poof—you're gone?

JOY
That's what I'm afraid of.

EDDIE

That wouldn't make much sense—would it?

JOY

Well ... no. Not really.

EDDIE

I mean, to just ... disappear ... vanish without a trace ... as if one never existed! It sounds a bit preposterous ... don't you think?

JOY

I ... I suppose it does.

EDDIE

I mean, where would one *go*?
[*A nervous little laugh.*]
Although, it ... it *is* very dark.
[*The beach has, indeed, grown quite dark. EDDIE seems to be growing frightened himself. There is only a small portion of beach that remains illuminated around the two of them.*]
I've never seen it so dark before. And so quiet. And it seems to be getting closer—the darkness. It's creeping up on us.
[*Pause.*]
Have you ever seen it so—

JOY
[*Attempting to suppress her rising terror.*]
Hold my hand!

                              EDDIE
All right!

> *[They cling to each other desperately as the
> darkness slowly envelops them.]*

                               JOY
I don't want to disappear!

                              EDDIE
You're not going to disappear!

                               JOY
I can't see my feet!

                              EDDIE
Just ... just keep talking!

> *[Only their faces are visible now.]*

                               JOY
What do I say?!

                              EDDIE
Anything!

                               JOY
All right!

                              EDDIE
As long as we keep talking, we should be—

> *[EDDIE vanishes.]*

JOY

Hello? *Hello?!*

     [Pause.]

Wasn't ... wasn't someone just ...

     [Pause.]

I thought I heard a voice. Is there anybody out there?

     [Pause.]

No?

     [Pause.]

I think there was someone else once ... a long time ago.

     [Pause.]

I remember a boy ... he bought me a dress ... a frilly thing with lots of lace ... he ... he said he was coming back for me but ... he never came.

     [Pause.]

He never came.

     [Pause.]

Hello?

     [She vanishes. Blackout.]

* * *

THE FATHER CLOCK

The Father Clock premiered at the University of Nevada, Las Vegas, on October 29, 1997, under the direction of Greg Vovos. The cast was as follows:

STAGE MANAGER: Sheilagh M. Polk
SNUB: Russ Marchand
FLUB: Doug Hill

SETTING:
A stage.

*[A bare stage. Shadows from the grid above.
Somewhere, the ticking of a clock. After a few
moments, a dim glow appears downstage center
and grows into a great pool of light. Silence
except for the ticking of the clock. More silence.
Finally, frantic whispering offstage left.]*

FLUB

Where is she?

SNUB

What?

FLUB

Where is she?!

SNUB

Who?

FLUB

The stage manager!
          *[The whispering rises, grows undecipherable. A
          heated exchange. A slap.]*

SNUB

Oww

          *[Pause. FLUB rushes across the stage, his face
          hidden beneath his jacket. He disappears into the
          wings—stage right. More whispering, urgent but
          undecipherable.]*

225

STAGE MANAGER

Breathe!

> *[Offstage right, FLUB takes in a great gulp of air.]*

Now go!

FLUB

But—

STAGE MANAGER

Go!

FLUB

All right! I don't think they suspect anything yet!
> *[Again, FLUB rushes across the stage, his jacket*
> *over his head. He disappears into the wings—*
> *stage left.]*

She's coming!

SNUB

What?

FLUB

She's coming!

SNUB

So?

> *[Another heated exchange as the STAGE*
> *MANAGER enters and steps into the pool of light.*
> *She is an attractive young woman, although a little*
> *out of sorts. Offstage, a slap.]*

FLUB

Oww!

STAGE MANAGER

Good evening, and welcome to—
> *[She sneezes.]*

Sorry. There's … ahh … there's something going around. A
little bug.
> *[She wipes her nose.]*

Welcome to the theatre. Now, before we get started, I'm afraid
we have a bit of bad news. The director won't be with us
tonight. He was called away suddenly. Several weeks ago.
> *[Pause.]*

Before rehearsals began, really.
> *[Pause.]*

Oh, no need to worry! I know many of you have come for his
fabled *mise en scène*, and you won't be disappointed! He did
supervise some table work! And we do have *this*—
> *[She produces a black prompt book.]*

—with a few scribbles from the director himself! Various notes.
 Suggestions and so forth. So stay for the show. We think you'll
find his hand at work in our little play. And if you must leave,
please slip out as quietly as possible. Without making too much
of a fuss. The actors, you know.
> *[Lights shift.]*

OK. That's it.
> *[She sneezes, takes her place on a stool stage right,*
> *and flips to the beginning of the prompt book.]*

The home of FLUB and SNUB DRUB. Four walls—deep olive.
> *[Lights rise to full on the empty stage.]*

NOTE FROM THE DIRECTOR: Four walls may or may not appear. Probably not.

> *[They do not.]*

A table, stage right. Two chairs.

> *[FLUB enters with a table and two chairs. SNUB wanders on behind him casually smoking a cigarette. FLUB drops his load stage right and carefully places each item in its proper place. SNUB flops down in one of the chairs. FLUB glares at him.]*

A couch.

> *[FLUB turns to exit. He pauses for a moment, expecting SNUB to follow, but he does not. Exit FLUB, glaring. He returns with a couch.]*

Brown.

> *[As FLUB's couch is not brown, he exits. He returns with a brown couch.]*

With four legs.

> *[As FLUB's couch has only three legs, he exits. He returns with a brown, four-legged couch.]*

Stage left.

> *[FLUB complies. SNUB puffs on his cigarette. The STAGE MANAGER watches carefully. When FLUB is finished, she continues.]*

A purple throw rug from Indonesia just downstage and to the right of the couch.

> *[FLUB glares at SNUB. He motions, "After you," but SNUB does not budge. Again, he motions, "After you." Again, SNUB does not budge. FLUB exits in a huff. He produces a rug and, with a*

> *flourish, places it in front of the couch.]*

A grandfather clock, upstage center.

> *[Exit FLUB. Offstage, a tremendous groan.*
> *FLUB reappears carrying a huge antique*
> *grandfather clock and places it upstage center. The*
> *clock has NO HANDS, but its pendulum is in*
> *motion and its steady ticking fills the auditorium.]*

This particular piece was procured by the director himself!

SNUB

Pfff!

> *[SNUB exits. The others glare after him.]*

STAGE MANAGER

SNUB DRUB enters as if from nowhere.

> *[SNUB DRUB enters—clearly from*
> *SOMEWHERE. He may be clawing his way out of*
> *some primordial muck, blowing kisses to a lover he*
> *has just left behind, running from some mythical*
> *beast with four heads and ten eyes, or perhaps all*
> *of these at once.]*

From nowhere.

> *[SNUB shrugs his shoulders and snorts.]*

From *nowhere*.

> *[SNUB ignores her—or perhaps continues with his*
> *pantomime.]*

SNUB DRUB enters as if—

SNUB

[*Nastily.*]

Trollop!

STAGE MANAGER

What's that?

SNUB

Pig-whore!

[*SNUB folds his arms and turns away from the
STAGE MANAGER. She approaches him.*]

STAGE MANAGER

Is there a *problem?*

SNUB

No!

STAGE MANAGER

No? No problem?

[*SNUB ignores her.*]

Then what was all of *this?*

[*She reenacts his entrance. SNUB shrugs.*]

SNUB

Nothing.

STAGE MANAGER

Nothing?

                    SNUB
I'm trying to establish the "moment before."

                    STAGE MANAGER
Ahh! The moment before!

                    SNUB
That's right.

                    STAGE MANAGER
Well, that's very considerate. But the note specifically states—
          [SNUB snorts and rolls his eyes.]
All right. That's enough. SNUB DRUB enters as if—

                    SNUB
          [Explodes.]
Why?! Why do I have to enter from *nowhere?!* What if I want
to enter from *somewhere?!*

                    STAGE MANAGER
It's not your place to question.

                    SNUB
Why not?!

                    STAGE MANAGER
An actor doesn't have to understand.

                    SNUB
Why not?!

STAGE MANAGER

It's not his place.

SNUB

Why not?!

STAGE MANAGER

Because!

SNUB

Because *why?!*

STAGE MANAGER

It's the director's job!

SNUB

Ah-hah! The *director!* I knew it'd come down to him!

STAGE MANAGER

Oh, just do it. We don't have time for—

SNUB

But it doesn't make any sense! Think about it! The way you used to! Take the whole clock thing—

STAGE MANAGER

Don't!

SNUB

Break it down!

STAGE MANAGER
Don't start about the clock! From nowhere!

SNUB
There's no logical explanation!

STAGE MANAGER
It's symbolic!

SNUB
Of what?!
    [Pause.]

STAGE MANAGER
From nowhere!

SNUB
You see! It doesn't make any—

STAGE MANAGER
[Reading from the prompt book.]
NOTE FROM THE DIRECTOR: It is most crucial that SNUB
enter as if from *nowhere!* Nothingness! Absolute non-
existence! The fact that he is, indeed, entering from somewhere
is irrelevant! Total nonsense! The important thing is that he's
here!
    [They glare at each other for a long moment.
    Finally, SNUB relents. He exits and returns a
    moment later as if from nowhere.]
Thank you.

SNUB
[Under his breath.]
He's lost his mind.

STAGE MANAGER
What's that?!

SNUB
Nothing.
[Pause. The STAGE MANAGER returns to her prompt book.]

STAGE MANAGER
SNUB wears a pleasant expression, although not so pleasant! A raspberry longing in his eyes. His hair is short and hangs to his waist. He is well built, although a little flabby and thin as a stick. His dress is not unusual. And he carries with him an ice cream cone—flavor optional.
[SNUB produces an ice cream cone.]
He flops down on the couch. Head stage right. Feet stage left. Belly up. One foot off. Cone in downstage hand.
[SNUB complies.]
Enter FLUB DRUB. He wheezes slightly.
[Enter FLUB, wheezing.]
Approximately 10 decibels please.
[FLUB complies.]
He looks much the same as SNUB—only older. In his left hand, he carries a pipe.
[FLUB produces a pipe.]

FLUB

<Snub … I call you Snub because that is your name. Snub Drub.>

STAGE MANAGER

SNUB licks his cone.

FLUB

<As you well know … I am your father.>

STAGE MANAGER

SNUB licks his cone!
> [He does.]

FLUB

<Please do not drip on this couch which we purchased only yesterday at approximately two a.m. in the freezing blizzard that is outside our pre-fabricated home in the northern portion of the United States of America—specifically North Dakota—although we are originally from Amarillo.>

STAGE MANAGER

A strange expression comes over SNUB that cannot be explained.
> [Indeed, it does.]

FLUB

<Son?>

                    SNUB
<Our couch!>

                    FLUB
<What's that?>

                    SNUB
<Our couch! Our couch!>

                    FLUB
<Ahh! Yes!>

                    SNUB
<I remember!>

                    FLUB
<The couch?>

                    SNUB
<The old one!>

                    FLUB
<Ahh! The old one!>

                    SNUB
<I remember when we bought it!>

                    FLUB
<Yesterday. When you were six.>

SNUB

<We went to the store-->

FLUB

<The store! That's right!>

SNUB

<--and we bought the couch!>

FLUB

<We bought it! Yes!>

SNUB

<You said, "Snub, do you think this couch will do?" And I said, "Yes, Father," for you are my father, "I think it will." I remember quite vividly. It was also brown-->

FLUB

<Like broccoli.>

SNUB

<--although not as comfortable.>

FLUB

<And with only three legs.>

SNUB

<My mother—your wife—who is now dead if you don't remember—loved that couch.>

*[The STAGE MANAGER sneezes. FLUB and
SNUB stare at her. She wipes her nose.]*

STAGE MANAGER

Oh … sorry … sorry … go ahead … I'm sorry … go on … just a
little cold.

SNUB

[Bitterly.]
Hah! A little cold!

FLUB

What's that she says?

SNUB

A cold!

FLUB

A cold! Ah!

SNUB

Strumpet!

FLUB

Trollop!

SNUB

Hussy!

FLUB

Wench!

SNUB

Where do you suppose she *caught* that cold?!

FLUB

That cold?

SNUB

Yes! "The cold!"

FLUB

Hmmm … let me think!

SNUB

The *old?*

FLUB

The *dying?!*

SNUB

The *sick?*

FLUB

Diseased?!

SNUB

Perhaps she shouldn't hump the lepers! Bang the bedridden!

STAGE MANAGER

It's just a little cold!

SNUB

A little cold, she says!

FLUB

Hah! A little cold!

STAGE MANAGER

DO YOU MIND?!

SNUB
[To FLUB. Quietly.]
A short temper. That's one of the first signs.

STAGE MANAGER
All right! That's it! Perhaps you'd like to muddle through on
your own! Perhaps I should just take the book and leave!

FLUB

No, wait—

SNUB

Go ahead.
*[SNUB pulls a cigarette from his pocket and lights
up.]*
Take the clock too, if you'd like. It's only confusing things.

> STAGE MANAGER

Oh! *It's* confusing things?!

> SNUB

That's right.

> FLUB

He's … he's only saying that. He doesn't mean it. *Do you?*
He's really quite fond of the clock. He's confided in me many
times just how … how fond of it he is. How it comforts him!
Nurtures him! Suckles him like a pig!
> *[SNUB snorts.]*

It's just … it's just … with his hard outer shell … you know …
it's so hard for him to admit.

> SNUB

We're better off without it.

> FLUB

Shut up!

> SNUB

Well, it's true.

> FLUB

No need to take chances!

> STAGE MANAGER

No smoking.

SNUB

What's that?

STAGE MANAGER

No smoking in the theatre.

SNUB

You never complained when *he* used to light up.

STAGE MANAGER

It was his theatre.

SNUB
[Jumps on this.]
Was? Did you say *was?!*

STAGE MANAGER
[Flustered.]
No ... I—

SNUB

"Was!" "Was his theatre!"

FLUB

We ... we should continue! Okay? Here ... here we go! We're moving on! We're ... we're, ahh ... c'mon ... we're ... we're not ...
[Pause.]
What would he think if he were to return and find us like this?! He could be making his way through the parking lot right now!

Wiping the smoke and dust from his spectacles! He … he could be in the lobby … his ear pressed to the door … listening! He'd be heartbroken! And besides …

> *[FLUB glances nervously into the auditorium.]*

I think they're getting restless.

> *[All three turn to the audience. An awkward pause.]*

STAGE MANAGER

You're right.

> *[The STAGE MANAGER flips through her prompt book. FLUB moves back to his place. SNUB takes a deep drag.]*

SNUB extinguishes his cigarette.

SNUB

It doesn't say—

STAGE MANAGER

SNUB extinguishes his cigarette!

> *[Pause.]*

SNUB

Fine.

> *[He extinguishes his cigarette and returns to his place.]*

That's all you understand anymore. Rules.

FLUB

[Continuing his performance.]
<As you know, Snub, I have called you here under the premise
of purchasing yet a third couch. Of course, I am slightly
untrustworthy, as you know, and there is the possibility this was
a ruse.>

SNUB

<That is always a possibility with you, Father. As you say, you
are slightly untrustworthy.>

FLUB

<Indeed.>

SNUB

<Take, for instance, the time you told me we were going to the
fair and instead you took me for a polio vaccination.>

FLUB

<Ah! Yes!>
[FLUB laughs maniacally.]

SNUB

<Or the spoon thing.>
[FLUB freezes.]

STAGE MANAGER

An awkward moment.
[Indeed.]

FLUB

<As … as you know, your mother—who is dead—>

SNUB

<What did she die of again?>

FLUB

<Polio.>

SNUB

<That's right. Do you remember when we bought this clock?>

FLUB

<Ah! The Father Clock!>

SNUB

<There was a saleswoman with dark red lipstick and large thighs. She wore a purple blouse.>

FLUB

<Yes! She gave you that cone!>

SNUB

<A black skirt. And her panty-line was quite visible. I remember noticing her panty-line. It was an important moment in my life. A sexual awakening, if you will.>

STAGE MANAGER

The clock strikes five.

*[At the sound of the clock, FLUB and SNUB
exchange positions on the stage. Each attempts to
replicate the other actor's last posture exactly.
FLUB now holds the cone. SNUB holds the pipe.]*

SNUB
[Mimics FLUB.]
<Yes ... she reminded me of your mother ... who is dead.>

FLUB
[Mimics SNUB.]
<What did she die of again?>

SNUB
<Polio.>

FLUB
<That's right.>

SNUB
<As you know, I have been alone all these years since your dear
mother—who is dead—died. Well ... feeling lonely, and having
no outlet for my ravenous sexual desires, I have decided to
remarry.>

FLUB
<Won't mother be jealous?>

SNUB
<Don't be ridiculous. She has her theatrical career.>

                    FLUB
<That's true.>

                    SNUB
<She's getting rave reviews!>

                    FLUB
<Yes … I've heard.>

                    SNUB
<Actually, I have remarried several times since her demise—
although I never told you.>

                    FLUB
<Indeed?>

                    SNUB
<Truly.>

                    FLUB
<Who will you marry this time, Father? I ask although I am
thrown slightly off balance by your sudden announcement.>

                    SNUB
<The woman who sold us the clock. With the red lipstick and
the panty line.>

                STAGE MANAGER
A strange contortion flits across FLUB's mackle.
            [Pause.]

FLUB
[To STAGE MANAGER.}
What's that?

STAGE MANAGER
A strange contortion flits across FLUB's mackle.

FLUB
Mackle?

STAGE MANAGER
Mackle.

FLUB
You're certain?
[The STAGE MANAGER scrunches up her nose,
presses the prompt book to her face.]

STAGE MANAGER
Yes. Mackle.

SNUB
[To the STAGE MANAGER.]
He's lost his mind. I told you.

FLUB
Let me see.

SNUB
I warned you, but you wouldn't listen.

STAGE MANAGER

Mackle.

SNUB

It's finally spread to his brain.
[She sneezes.]

FLUB

Hmmm …

STAGE MANAGER

Flits across his mackle!

SNUB

He's probably wandered off in a blind stupor. *That's* where he is. He's probably sitting on a corner somewhere, drooling on his trousers, babbling nonsense and—

FLUB

Shhh! What are you—

SNUB

—and if I recall correctly, it all started with a little cold!
[The STAGE MANAGER sneezes.]
Bless you.
[SNUB and FLUB stare at her. She wipes her nose.]

STAGE MANAGER

You're jealous!

FLUB
[Extremely agitated.]
Yes! Jealous!

SNUB
Hah!

STAGE MANAGER
You're such a child sometimes.

FLUB
Yes! A child!

STAGE MANAGER
You don't understand the way things are at all.

FLUB
Not at all!

SNUB
A *child?*

STAGE MANAGER
That's right.

FLUB
He ... he was called away! *Remember?!*

SNUB
Trollop!

FLUB
[Offers SNUB the prompt book, a distraction.]
What … ahh—

SNUB
Jezebel!

FLUB
—what do you make of this? This here.
[FLUB shoves the book at SNUB.]
It's handwritten. Encrypted. Takes a precise eye.
[As SNUB leans reluctantly over the prompt book,
the back of his shirt bulges out. FLUB notices this,
knocks on the bulge. There is the sound of
something solid. SNUB jerks away.]

SNUB
Don't touch that!

FLUB
What is it?

SNUB
Nothing! It's none of your business!
[FLUB tries to get a good look at the bulge, but
SNUB uses the prompt book to keep him at a
distance.]
Stay back! I'm warning you!
[Keeping a watchful eye on FLUB, SNUB studies
the prompt book.]

I'd have to say this is ... ahh—

STAGE MANAGER

Mackle!

[The STAGE MANAGER grabs the prompt book from SNUB. She returns SNUB and FLUB to their places.]

Go on!

FLUB

<Who ... ahh ... who will you marry this time, Father? I ask although I am thrown slightly off balance by your sudden announcement.>

SNUB

<The woman who sold us the clock. With the red lipstick and the panty line.>

STAGE MANAGER

A strange contortion flits across FLUB's *mackle!*
       [It does.]

SNUB

<I am a little concerned now over your pending reaction— although not too much.>

FLUB

[Menacingly.]
<Ahh! The woman who sold us the clock!>

STAGE MANAGER

A Pinter silence.
> *[Silence. FLUB and SNUB square off.]*

FLUB

<I must admit, I feel a bit betrayed and hurt that you could arrive at such an important decision without first consulting me— you're second but only living son.>

SNUB

<It couldn't be helped.>

STAGE MANAGER

Mackle grackle.
> *[Indeed.]*

FLUB

<Fortunately, I have news of my own, and this keeps me from losing my balance entirely. As you know, I have inherited your shifty and not entirely trustworthy disposition—along with your ravenous sexual desires. I, too, have decided to take a wife.>

SNUB

<I am feeling surprise.>

FLUB

<Good!>

SNUB

<A little shock … and yet pride that you—my second but only living son—find yourself comfortable speaking to me so openly about such intimate matters.>

FLUB

<Yes, well, as you know, you have raped me daily since my seventh birthday.>

SNUB

<Yes. That's true.>

FLUB

<So it is surprising that I would be this forthcoming. And yet I felt it necessary to inform you … I too am marrying the woman who sold us the clock. With the red lipstick and the panty-line.>

STAGE MANAGER
*[Presses the prompt book close to her face.
Scrunches her nose.]*
Danger … danger … hangs on the … bear … like a … truffle.
[FLUB and SNUB exchange an awkward glance.]
The cook strikes three.
*[Indeed, it does—the clock, that is. FLUB and
SNUB exchange places.]*

FLUB

<Now I am really surprised.>

SNUB

<Flub Drubby Drub!>

FLUB

<A little angry at your insolence—although not too much because of the guilt I feel over our sexual encounters—and yet happy in a strange sort of manic way.>

SNUB

<I'm glad we worked this out.>

FLUB

<As am I.>

STAGE MANAGER

Knockle tart.

SNUB

[To FLUB, after a concerned glance at the STAGE MANAGER.]

<Well … as you know, I must to work within the hour—in the freezing blizzard—to hawk my wares. Although I don't really need to leave for another thirty minutes or so, I believe I will go now because of a rising fear that you may want to pork me if I stick around.>

FLUB

<You're very alert, son.>

SNUB

<Goodbye, Father.>

FLUB

<Have a seat.>

SNUB

<Must I?>

FLUB

<Yes. Over here.>
        [SNUB sits. FLUB puts a hand on his son's knee.]

STAGE MANAGER

SNUB in barging flittle snorkel gum.
        *[SNUB and FLUB steal another glance at the
        STAGE MANAGER. She sneezes. Then, all at
        once, FLUB is overcome with a spasm of
        understanding, a great rush of knowledge. He
        rises, transfixed, little gurgling sounds coming from
        his throat.]*

SNUB

What?
        [More gurgling.]
What?! What is it?! What's wrong?!

FLUB

At … at last!

                    SNUB
What?

                    FLUB
At last! I understand my role! I'm fleshing it out!

                    SNUB
Really?!

                    FLUB
Yes! It's all clear to me now! His vision!

                    SNUB
          [Disbelief.]
No!

                    FLUB
Yes!

                    SNUB
Everything?

                    FLUB
Yes!

                    SNUB
What about the clock?!

                    FLUB
Yes!

SNUB

The clock too?!

FLUB

Yes!

SNUB

My god!

FLUB

Yes!

SNUB
[To the STAGE MANAGER.]
A pen! Quick! Something to write with!

STAGE MANAGER

I ...

SNUB

Hurry! Before he forgets!

STAGE MANAGER

I know there's ... wait ... I ... I remember once ... a long time
ago ... a ... a truffle ... a little chocolate bribe—
[SNUB snatches a pen from her.]

SNUB

Paper!

STAGE MANAGER

I ... I don't want to.

SNUB

What?

STAGE MANAGER

I don't want to anymore. You can't make me.

SNUB
[Reaching for the prompt book.]
Just tear a page from the—

STAGE MANAGER

No!
[She clutches the prompt book to her chest.]

SNUB

This is no time for—

STAGE MANAGER
[Terrified, a mother protecting her child.]
No!

SNUB

Oh for crying out ... fine!
*[SNUB rushes to FLUB, offers him the pen, and
holds out his other palm as a tablet.]*
Here! Use my hand!

FLUB

What?

SNUB

My hand! I brought you a pen!

FLUB

Oh. Thank you.
          [FLUB takes the pen and puts it in his pocket.]

SNUB

What are you doing?!

FLUB

Hmmm?

SNUB

The pen!

FLUB

What?

SNUB

The pen! I gave you a pen!

FLUB

Oh.

SNUB

Hurry!

[SNUB holds out his hand as a tablet.]

FLUB

You know … you really shouldn't give things away if you're not going to let people keep them.
          [FLUB puts the pen in SNUB's outstretched palm.]

SNUB

No! No! You had a revelation!

FLUB

A revelation?

SNUB

Yes!

FLUB

Did I?

SNUB

Yes! You were going to write it down for me! His vision! You said you'd figured it all out! Put it all together!

FLUB

All of it?

SNUB

Yes!

FLUB

What about the clock?

SNUB

Yes!

FLUB

The clock too?

SNUB

Yes!

FLUB

My god!

SNUB

Yes!

FLUB

I must have forgotten.

SNUB

Damn!
            [SNUB flops down on the couch.]
I almost had it!

FLUB

Had what?

SNUB

Nothing. It's none of your business.

> *[The clock strikes nine. FLUB stands and moves to the opposite end of the couch. He sits. SNUB glares at the STAGE MANAGER as she prostrates herself in front of the clock, the prompt book still clutched to her chest. FLUB takes SNUB's hand and places it on his knee. Pause.]*

FLUB

> *[Prompting SNUB.]*

"Don't be frightened, son."

> *[Pause. SNUB continues to glare at the STAGE MANAGER.]*

"Don't be frightened, son."

SNUB

> *[Reluctantly.]*

<Don't be frightened, son.>

FLUB

<I'm not, but what of our bride?>

SNUB

<Ah … *that*.>

FLUB

<The Gumbah.>

SNUB
<There's only one thing to do.>
                    [They thumb-wrestle.]

STAGE MANAGER

His ...
his long arm
dangling

dangling

rocking slightly

tick

tock

tick

tock

SNUB
<I win.>

FLUB
<You cheated! Your thumb is too long!>

SNUB
<It couldn't be helped.>

FLUB

<Two out of three!>

SNUB

<If you insist.>
[They thumb-wrestle.]

STAGE MANAGER

his weight

I am not afraid
I am not afraid
I am not afraid

his long arm
dangling
[SNUB wins.]

FLUB

<It's monstrous! You're a freak! A mutant! Three out of five!>

STAGE MANAGER

pounding
I am not afraid
pounding
[FLUB loses.]

FLUB

<Four out of seven!>

STAGE MANAGER

down
down
down

his long arm
pounding

my world
changed
rearranged
      with
           each
                  fantastic
                        blow
    [FLUB loses again.]

FLUB

<Damn!>

STAGE MANAGER

my world

the same

rearranged

always
the
same

FLUB

<There's no point to it! The cards are stacked!>
> *[The clock strikes one. The STAGE MANAGER*
> *panics at the sound of the clock. She dives under*
> *the table. SNUB and FLUB exchange places.]*

<I am VICTORIOUS! Hah!>
> *[FLUB takes SNUB by the ear and leads him to the*
> *STAGE MANAGER.]*

<Son, meet your mother. The woman who sold us the clock!>

SNUB

<Hello … mother.>

STAGE MANAGER
[Clinging to the table, terrified.]

mackle
mackle grackle
mackle grackle korpal fie
> *[Pause.]*

FLUB

What … what's wrong with her?
> *[SNUB kneels on the floor. FLUB follows.]*

What is it? Is … is she all right?
> *[To the STAGE MANAGER.]*

Are you all right?
> *[No response.]*

I think she's all right. She's just taking a breather.

SNUB
[To the STAGE MANAGER.]
Come here.
          [She does not move.]
Come on. It's all right ... I won't hurt you.
          *[SNUB reaches for her, but she lashes out
          violently.]*

STAGE MANGER
Korpal fie!
          [SNUB backs away.]

SNUB
She's lost her mind.

FLUB
No ...

SNUB
It's the old man that did it! The bastard!

STAGE MANAGER
          [To herself.]
I am not afraid
I am not afraid
I am not afraid

SNUB
I warned her, but she wouldn't listen! I knew what he was after!
What he wanted!

FLUB

It … it's just a little cold.

SNUB

I saw through him from the beginning! All of his *exercises!* His *rules!* He took advantage of her dedication! Of his position! He took advantage of us all! Corrupted us in his image!

FLUB
[Continuing the play.]
<She'll be a good mother.>

SNUB

WHAT?!!!

FLUB
<She'll … she'll be a good mother.>

SNUB

How can you go on?! LOOK AT HER! Look! Is that how you want to end up?! Is it?! Don't you see what he's doing?!
[FLUB covers his ears.]
He wants to keep us eternally beneath him!

FLUB

I can't hear you!

SNUB
Idiot children forever worshipping at his feet!

FLUB

I'm completely deaf!

SNUB

Feeding his overgrown ego!

FLUB

You might as well be talking to a pole!

SNUB

As soon as we get comfortable in one role, we have to take on
another! Why?!

FLUB

<She'll be a good mother.>

SNUB

Because he wants to keep us off balance! That's why! Because
he doesn't want us to THINK! He doesn't want us to
QUESTION HIS AUTHORITY! So he keeps us busy! Keeps
us running in circles! Like mice! Rushing from one role to the
next! Well, I'm on to his game! I see what he's doing! And I
refuse to participate!

> *[SNUB plants himself firmly on the couch. He folds*
> *his arms. FLUB looks around for a moment,*
> *panicked, then decides to play both roles.]*

FLUB
[As himself.]
<She'll be a good mother.>
[As SNUB.]
<In her fashion.>
[As himself.]
<She'll do the best she can.>
[As SNUB.]
<Will she tuck me in at night? And comfort me when I'm frightened? And feed me sugar plums? And read me stories until I fall asleep nestled between her breasts?>
[As himself.]
<Of course! Tell the boy a story!>
[FLUB pries the STAGE MANAGER from the table.]
Go on.

[He nudges her towards SNUB, but she keeps her distance, glaring suspiciously, half-crouched.]

STAGE MANAGER
In …

FLUB
That's it.

STAGE MANAGER
In the … the … beginning …

FLUB
Ah! The old standard! Go on!

STAGE MANAGER

In …

FLUB

In the beginning …

STAGE MANAGER

In the beginning …
> *[The STAGE MANAGER stands frozen, her eyes*
> *wide, ready to bolt at the slightest movement.*
> *Pause. FLUB turns to the audience.]*

FLUB

She tells it so well! She puts just the right emphasis! Go on!
> *[Pause.]*

Go on.

STAGE MANAGER

In the beginning …
> *[Another pause. She glares at SNUB suspiciously.]*

FLUB

In the beginning, everything was wonderful! Fine! Okay, skip
ahead! Let's have the juicy part! The climax!

STAGE MANAGER

In the …

FLUB

The last …

STAGE MANAGER
[Agitated.]
The last ... days ...

FLUB

That's it!

STAGE MANAGER

The final ... hours ... the ... the clock ... struck ...

FLUB

Ah! The clock!

STAGE MANAGER

Struck ...

FLUB

The clock struck twelve!

STAGE MANAGER

His long arm ... pounding ...

FLUB

And then? What happened next?!
[SNUB and the STAGE MANAGER glare at one
another, motionless. Silence.]

STAGE MANAGER

Nothing.

FLUB

N … *nothing?*
>   *[A nervous little laugh.]*
There must be *something!*

STAGE MANAGER
>   *[Staring deep into SNUB's soul.]*
No. Darkness.
>   *[SNUB glares back at her. The clock strikes four.]*

FLUB

Damn this eternal flip-flop!

STAGE MANAGER
>   *[Enraptured, prostrating herself in front of the*
>   *clock.]*
It's … his vision!

SNUB

To hell with his vision!

FLUB

What?

SNUB

To hell with his vision! That's right! He isn't here to see it
through! What about *our* vision?!

FLUB

We … we don't have any! We're not allowed!

                    SNUB
Why not?!

                    FLUB
Shhh! Not so—

                    SNUB
Not so loud?! I hope he *does* hear!

                    FLUB
But he … he *MADE* you!

                    SNUB
And where is he *NOW?! Huh?!*

                    FLUB
You were NOTHING!

                    STAGE MANAGER
          [Childlike, an exploration of her own little world.]
Clay …

                    FLUB
An unknown!

                    STAGE MANAGER
Dirt …

FLUB

He taught you everything! Took you under his wing! Educated
you!

SNUB

Hah!

FLUB

You were like a son to him!

STAGE MANAGER

Sand …

SNUB

And when it comes down to the wire, he's nowhere to be
found—is he?! Vanished into thin air! The great director!

STAGE MANAGER
[Feeling her stomach.]

Lumpy …

FLUB

Without him, you're lost! You're nothing! A second-rate actor!
A child!

STAGE MANAGER

A …

SNUB

I AM NOT A CHILD!

STAGE MANAGER

A child …

FLUB

The best you can do is follow! Blindly! You can't grasp it!
You can't get your mind around it!

STAGE MANAGER
[Feeling her belly. A grand discovery.]

A child!

FLUB

It's beyond you!

STAGE MANAGER

Oh! A clay baby!
*[The STAGE MANAGER rubs her belly, delighted.
A soft little laugh. SNUB and FLUB watch,
dumbstruck.]*

FLUB

She … she's not …
*[The STAGE MANAGER grabs her belly feeling a
little kick for the first time.]*

STAGE MANAGER

Oh!

FLUB

No! She ... she can't be! He couldn't have! Could he? He's ...
he's beyond that!

SNUB

The bastard!

FLUB

He ... he must have had some reason! Some purpose! A ... a
greater plan!

SNUB

Hah!

FLUB

Everything happens for a reason! It's not our place to question!
It will all come clear in the end!

STAGE MANAGER

In me
there is order

in my body
meaning

I hold the secret

here

traces
left behind
fragments
shadows

fill in the blank

I am a rune
a carrot
a little joke

I am the Moon

No man can ever know
never know me
possess me

SNUB

But I have.

STAGE MANAGER

You haven't.

SNUB

I have. I've known you.

STAGE MANAGER

No … you only thought you had!

SNUB

Listen to me! Listen! Your ... your mind is clouded right now.
Okay? You're not thinking clearly. We have to get away from
here. That's all. Away from *him!* And then everything will fall
back into place! Like a dream! Like ... like waking up and
finding what's real!

> *[Pause.]*

I found an old play.

> *[He pulls a very old, cloth-covered book from his
> shirt.]*

It's one you've never read. It was supposed to have been burned
years ago—along with all of its kind—it didn't fit the director's
vision. But somehow ... it survived! An original copy! I found
it in an old bookstore! They didn't know what they had! I ... I
was waiting to give it to you ... waiting for just the right
moment ... but now ... now I ... ... here.

> *[He offers her the book. She glares at him.]*

Please ... please take it.

> *[Pause.]*

Please?

> *[Pause.]*

We'll ... we'll read it together. Okay? It will open your eyes to
a ... a whole new world! A whole new language of the stage! A
forgotten language! We'll ... we'll talk about what it means ...
about ... about our real feelings. We'll have meaningful
discussions. And ... and one day ... we'll wake up ... and
everything will be just ... just like it used to be.

> *[The STAGE MANAGER takes the book from
> SNUB. Sniffs it.]*

STAGE MANAGER

A truffle.

SNUB

What? No …

STAGE MANAGER

A little chocolate bribe.

SNUB

No. That … that was a long time ago.
     [Pause.]
Am I never to be forgiven? Am I to be eternally punished for
one little indiscretion? One childish blunder?

STAGE MANAGER

Always the same.

SNUB

No! No, not always the same! Not always the same! I've
served my penance! I've done everything I could to make up for
it! Suffered countless humiliations! Groveled at your feet!
What more do you want from me?! Haven't I suffered enough?!
     [Pause.]
I can save you.
     [Pause.]
Are you willing to sacrifice your own happiness just to spite me?
     [She drops the book. SNUB picks it up.]
Don't … don't do this. Listen. Listen to me. He was a false
prophet. You have to wipe him out of your—

[He reaches for her.]

STAGE MANAGER
[Violently.]
Korpal fie!

[SNUB rises. Backs away. She sneezes. Wipes her nose. Sneezes again. Rubs her belly. A soft, little laugh. Silence. SNUB tosses the old book to the ground. He picks up one of the chairs and smashes it to the ground as well, breaking it into pieces. He picks up a jagged, heavy piece of wood. Brandishes it.]

FLUB
What ... what are you doing?!

SNUB
He's taken her away from me! Brainwashed her completely!
[FLUB throws himself in front of the STAGE MANAGER.]

FLUB
Stay back! I'm warning you!
[SNUB takes a step towards them.]

SNUB
What?

FLUB
Stay away from her! I ... I won't allow it!

SNUB

Not her.

FLUB

[Uneasily.]

Not … not her?

SNUB

No.

*[Pause. FLUB throws himself in front of the
clock.]*

FLUB

Don't come any closer!

SNUB

Get out of the way.

FLUB

Perhaps … perhaps he will return!

SNUB

No.

FLUB

Perhaps he's on his way! This very moment! Perhaps he's here!
Let's have a look!

[FLUB drags SNUB to the edge of the stage.]

SNUB

Let go of me!

> [*FLUB peers into the audience. Examines each face.*]

FLUB

No. No. No. No. No.

SNUB

You're wasting your time!

FLUB

No. No. No. No.

SNUB

He isn't coming back!

FLUB

No. No. No.

SNUB

Perhaps he's dead already! Did you think of that?!

FLUB

No!

SNUB

And if he *does* show his face, I'll break it in two! I'll smash his brains in!

[FLUB spots something in the auditorium. He stares hard.]

FLUB

Is that … there … in the … … it's him!

SNUB

What?

FLUB

It's him! It's him! He's come back! He's returned! At last! We're saved!

[SNUB steps forward, brandishing his weapon.]

SNUB

Where?

STAGE MANAGER

At last!

FLUB

There!

SNUB

Where?!

FLUB

There!

STAGE MANAGER

At last!

SNUB

I can't see!

FLUB

There! In the last row!

SNUB

The last row?!

FLUB

We're saved!

SNUB

There?!

FLUB

Yes!

SNUB

Right there?

FLUB

Yes!

[SNUB peers into the audience.]

SNUB

It isn't him.

FLUB

It is!

SNUB

No.

FLUB

Shut up! You're insane!

SNUB
[Bitterly.]
Ask *her* if you don't believe me! She ought to know!
[The STAGE MANAGER sneezes.]

FLUB
[To the STAGE MANAGER.]
Well?

[FLUB leads the STAGE MANAGER to the front of the stage. There is a long, hopeful silence as she stares into the audience. The clock strikes twelve. After a moment, she lowers her head and turns away.]

Well?
[Pause.]
Did you see him or didn't you?
[Pause.]
Didn't you?
[The STAGE MANAGER grows agitated, begins to moan softly.]
What? What is it? What's wrong?

SNUB

It ... it's stopped.

FLUB

What?

[SNUB points to the clock. It's pendulum stands still. There is only silence.]

It's ...

[He approaches the clock. Touches it.]

It's ... no ... no, it can't ...

[To SNUB.]

What have you done?!

SNUB

I didn't touch it.

FLUB

It can't be!

[FLUB tries to set the pendulum in motion. At his touch, however, the clock collapses. Falls to pieces.]

What ... what does this mean?! What does it mean?! I don't ... I don't understand!

[FLUB tries desperately to rebuild the clock, but only makes things worse.]

No! How ... how could he leave us?! Now! When we need him most! He ... he said he'd always be here! Until the end of time! He ...

[FLUB turns to the clock, terrified.]

... he promised.

[Pause.]
And now … he's … it's all … it's all falling apart … and he's
not … he's not here to … to put it all …
[Pause.]
WHERE IS HE?!
[Pause.]
He must … he must be on his way! He's been held up! That's
all! Caught in traffic! The streets are empty, I admit, but … all
of those lights … some of them still work, and he's … he's
probably … oh wait … I've got it! He's found another theatre!
That's it! A new space! And he wanted to surprise us! Oh, how
exciting! We've been acting like such babies! He'll have a
good laugh at our expense, won't he! I can't wait to see! A new
stage! It must be something wonderful! Not like this one! This
husk! No! This is only a shadow! A mustard seed! Why it's …
it's probably beyond our ability to grasp! Something
magnificent for once! A … a single site! With no partition! No
barrier! No auditorium!
*[FLUB jumps down from the stage and into the
audience.]*
One space! All of us together! A hundred thousand swiveling
seats! Always a full house! And lots of clapping! Clapping and
laughter! And … and lights! Oh! Lights! All kinds of
luminous vibrations! Fresnels of gold shooting light in waves, in
sheets, in fusillades of fiery arrows! A living theatre! It's going
to be something! He must be on his way! Right now! To tell
us! To let us know! I'm going to tell him all of the silly ideas
we've passed around! We'll all have a good laugh! All of us!
A nice little chuckle! He's … he's probably at the door right
now! There! That cough! Did you hear it?! I'd know that

cough anywhere! We have to give him a great welcome!
>   *[FLUB throws open the doors of the theatre, but*
>   *there is no one there. Pause.]*
I ... I don't ...

STAGE MANAGER
>   *[To herself.]*
Alone.

>   *[She lies on the floor and begins to babble*
>   *nonsense as she rocks back and forth. SNUB*
>   *stands over her as FLUB makes his way back to the*
>   *stage. Silence.]*

FLUB
I've ... I've made a great fool of myself. Haven't I?

SNUB
It doesn't matter.
>   *[Pause.]*

FLUB
What ... ahh ... what ... what happens now?

SNUB
Now?
>   *[Pause.]*
Nothing. Darkness.
>   *[SNUB pulls a cigarette from his pocket. Lights it.]*

FLUB

How ... how can you be sure?

SNUB

I'm sure.
> *[A deep drag.]*

We're free at last.

FLUB

Free?

SNUB

That's right.
> *[Pause.]*

Our penance is over.
> *[Silence.]*

FLUB

What ... what's that?

SNUB

What?

FLUB

That. Listen.
> *[Somewhere, the sound of a clock can be heard ticking ever so faintly.]*

SNUB

Echoes.

                    FLUB
No ...

*[FLUB examines the remains of the clock, but they
are silent. The ticking grows louder. FLUB begins
to circle the stage. Gradually, he zeroes in on the
STAGE MANAGER. He circles her. Puts an ear to
her belly. His eyes grow wide.]*
My god!

                    SNUB
What?

                    FLUB
Listen!

            [SNUB does not move.]

                    SNUB
What?

                    FLUB
Go on!

            [SNUB does not budge.]

                    SNUB
It can't be.

                    FLUB
It is!

SNUB

But—

FLUB

Listen!

[Still, SNUB does not move.]

SNUB

It … it wouldn't make any sense.

FLUB

I'm telling you!

*[The ticking grows louder. The STAGE MANAGER
giggles as FLUB pokes her belly.]*

It's a miracle! I knew he'd make arrangements!

SNUB

It can't be! There's … there's no logical explanation!

FLUB

So what! Mackle grackle!

*[FLUB begins to hop madly about the stage,
clapping wildly.]*

Mackle grackle korpal fie! Korpal fie! Korpal fie!

SNUB

She … she can't have a *clock* inside her! What kind of sense
would that make?! It's ridiculous!

*[The STAGE MANAGER grabs her belly—another
kick.]*

STAGE MANAGER

Oh!

FLUB

We'll ... we'll raise it as our own! A wolf cub! A ... a child of the theatre!

SNUB

What?

FLUB

Someone has to take responsibility! The director's gone, and ... and she's near the end. I'm sorry, but it's true. You might as well face up to it. She doesn't have much time left. We'll have to watch her so she doesn't wander off. This is going to be exciting! A real adventure! I'll ... I'll nurture the child! Comfort it! Generations will call me blessed!

SNUB

You?

FLUB

Yes!

SNUB

What kind of father would *you* make?!

FLUB

Do you have a better idea?

> *[FLUB puts a hand on the STAGE MANAGER's belly.]*

STUB ... I call you STUB because that is your name. STUB DRUB.

SNUB

Are you blind?! It's another trick! That's all it is! Another illusion to distract you!

> *[The STAGE MANAGER cries out. This time, however, she grabs her stomach in pain.]*

STAGE MANAGER

Oh!

> *[She freezes, startled by the pain. Fear in her eyes, she turns to FLUB.]*

FLUB

It ... it's trying to tell us something!

SNUB

The *clock-thing?* The *mutant?*

FLUB

Yes! Maybe—

STAGE MANAGER

> *[Clearly in pain.]*

Oh!

FLUB

My god! It … it's coming!

SNUB

What?

FLUB

It's coming! The child is coming!

STAGE MANAGER

The child!

SNUB

It can't be!

FLUB

Yes! The child!

STAGE MANAGER

The child!

SNUB

Look, whatever that … that *thing* is … it's not a child! Don't let it fool you! It's been around forever! Since the beginning of time! In some deep, dark hole somewhere! Some chasm! Just waiting for some poor fool like you to come along and set it free!

     [The STAGE MANAGER grimaces, her pains growing stronger.]

STAGE MANAGER

Oh!

SNUB

It's going to grow into another tyrant! You know that! Some
great beast trampling everything in its path!

STAGE MANAGER

In … in me there is order!

FLUB

Yes!

SNUB

Another Caesar! Or worse!

FLUB

Order!

SNUB

I won't allow it!

STAGE MANAGER

In my body!

FLUB

That's right!

SNUB

I can't!

STAGE MANAGER

Meaning!

SNUB

I'll fight it 'til the end!
> [Once again, FLUB is overcome with a sudden
> rush of knowledge, little gurgling sounds come up
> out of his throat. He gestures wildly at SNUB,
> horrified.]

What? What is it?

FLUB

I know you!

SNUB

Of course you know me.

FLUB

No! I ... I *know* you! I know who you are! I see through your disguise!

SNUB

My *disguise?*

FLUB

Yes!

SNUB

You've known me since I was a child.
> *[FLUB grabs a piece of wood from the broken
> chair and brandishes it.]*

What's gotten into you?

FLUB

Stay back!

SNUB

What?

FLUB

Stay away from her!

SNUB

All right. Look. Why don't you just sit down for a minute?
Okay? Sit down. Take a deep breath. Try to relax. And let me
take care of this.

FLUB

Don't come any closer! I'm warning you!
> *[FLUB lunges at SNUB, brandishing his weapon.
> The STAGE MANAGER cries out in pain.]*

SNUB

She needs help.

FLUB

I'll help her!

[FLUB kneels beside the STAGE MANAGER.]

Breathe.

[She does.]

That's it. Take my hand.

*[She takes his hand and squeezes hard as she cries
out.]*

Okay. That's it. Okay. Okay, not *quite* so hard!

[The STAGE MANAGER cries out.]

I ... I see a ... a foot! No ... something ... not a foot, but a ... a
... a shoulder perhaps? Or a knee? Maybe a very small bottom?
Something with a little curve to it ...

[The STAGE MANAGER cries out.]

Push!

[Again, the STAGE MANAGER cries out.]

What? What's wrong? What is it? Are you in pain? Here!
Squeeze my hand!

[She begins to sob.]

What? Is something wrong?

[Pause.]

Oh god ... oh god ... it's ... I ... I think it's ... it's stuck! The
... the child is stuck! What do we do now?! I don't want to hurt
her! Breathe! I ... I didn't expect complications!

*[FLUB retrieves the prompt book. Flips through it,
desperately searching for instructions of some
sort.]*

I ... I don't ... I don't know what to do!

[Another cry.]

Oh god, she's in pain! Help me!

[SNUB laughs, delighted. He takes the prompt book from FLUB.]

SNUB

Very good!
[SNUB applauds.]

FLUB

What?!

SNUB

Very good. That's a nice moment.

FLUB

How can you—

SNUB

[Scribbling something in the prompt book.]
Okay … take five.

FLUB

What?

SNUB

Take five.
[Pause.]
It's the final step. The only logical conclusion.
[SNUB exits, still scribbling, his mind racing, the cigarette dangling from his lips. FLUB looks a little befuddled.]

FLUB

What ... ahh ... what ... what did he mean by that? That last remark?

[The STAGE MANAGER cries out. FLUB tries to comfort her.]

STAGE MANAGER

I am a carrot!

FLUB

Yes.

STAGE MANAGER

A little joke!

[She bursts into hysterical laughter which degenerates into a long, painful sob. FLUB holds his head as if it might explode, begins to scurry about the stage like a mouse.]

FLUB

He ... he's really quite fond of the clock! He's confided in me many times just how ... how fond of it he is! How it comforts him! Nurtures him! Suckles him like a—

[The STAGE MANAGER cries out, much louder than before. FLUB is drawn to her, cringing. He pauses.]

It's ...

[Again, she cries out. FLUB moves closer.]

It's ... it's coming! It's coming! Isn't it?!

[She nods through the pain.]

My god! It's coming! Push! That's it! I ... I can't believe it's
... it's really ... it's a miracle!

>   *[She cries out.]*

Good! That's it! Almost there! We're getting closer! One!
Last!

>   *[One great final scream. The STAGE MANAGER
>   collapses from exhaustion. FLUB rises from
>   between the STAGE MANAGER's legs. In his
>   hands he holds a ringing alarm clock.]*

... time.

>   *[As the lights begin their final fade to black, they
>   linger for a moment on FLUB. Befuddled and
>   alone. With his clock ringing into the darkness.]*

* * *

CPSIA information can be obtained at www.ICGtesting.com
Printed in the USA
LVOW06s1050271013

358731LV00001B/294/P